Saige

Paints the Sky

by Jessie Haas

★ American Girl®

For Tiff, Kristina, and Julianna—Jo's precious girls

Questions or comments? Call 1-800-845-0005, visit **americangirl.com**, or write to
Customer Service, American Girl, 8400 Fairway Place, Middleton, WI 53562-0497.

Printed in China
13 14 15 16 17 18 19 20 LEO 10 9 8 7 6 5 4 3 2 1

All American Girl marks and Saige™ are trademarks of American Girl.

Illustrations by Sarah Davis

Real Girls, Real Stories adapted and reprinted from *American Girl* magazine; "Hold Your
Own Craft Sale" tips adapted from *Express Yourself* by Emma MacLaren Henke, illustrated
by Charlie Alder.

Special thanks to Beth Larsen, Executive Director of Art in the School, Albuquerque, NM,
and Randy Cohen, Vice President of Research and Policy, Americans for the Arts.

Cataloging-in-Publication Data available from the Library of Congress.

Contents

"So, how'd it go? Did everyone like the pictures you put up?" asked Mom as I hopped into the car beside her.

It was Monday afternoon, and we were heading over to the rehab center to see my grandma Mimi, who'd broken her leg and wrist a few weeks earlier.

Just this morning, my friend Gabi and I had gone to school early to decorate the hallways with drawings that kids had made during our fund-raising fiesta for the arts. We were trying to raise money for an after-school arts program, since my school couldn't afford to offer art this year.

"Everyone *loved* the drawings!" I said. "And they're really excited about the after-school art class. When is the PTA going to get that going?"

"It's not that simple, Saige," Mom said. "We still need to find a few art teachers and other volunteers to help supervise the kids—and this may come as news to you, darling, but teachers have lives, too!"

Of course that wasn't news to me. Mom's a teacher—well, a college math professor, but it's the same thing. I knew that teachers had kids of their own to go home to, horses to ride, ranches to run, and homework to correct . . . *our* homework! Hey, that was an idea.

"If they gave us less homework, they'd have more free time," I suggested.

Mom ignored that.

I spoke up again—I couldn't help it. "We just want an art class. *One art class!* Is that too much to ask?"

Mom sighed. "It depends on *how* you ask," she said. "We're feeling our way forward, Saige, and it's going to take time."

I could tell by the tone of her voice that the PTA really was trying, and that meant it really would take time. I got a sinking feeling in the pit of my stomach. I couldn't help saying, "It's taken a lot of time already."

"I know," Mom said, reaching over to squeeze my knee. "But in the meantime, you can paint at Mimi's." My grandmother is a professional painter, and until she got hurt, I spent every afternoon at her *ranchita*, riding horses or painting in her studio. Mimi would be out of rehab soon, and at least the painting part of our afternoons would start again.

But what about Gabi? I wondered. *What about the other kids at school?* Nobody else got to paint every day after school like I did. I was grateful for what I had, but I felt a little guilty, too.

We found Mimi in the commons room, with

2

a group of people all laughing and talking at once. Most of the patients were Mimi's age or older, but the scene reminded me of the school cafeteria at lunchtime—friendly and fun.

Mimi caught sight of us. "Good!" she said, getting slowly to her feet and reaching for her walker. She was using a specially built walker so that she could put weight on her elbow, not her broken wrist. It made her seem clumsy—*Mimi*, who trained and rode horses and had even been dusting off her trick-riding skills just a month ago.

Mom and I walked with Mimi back to her room—that is, Mom walked with her. I kept zooming ahead every few steps and having to stop myself and wait. Mimi was so slow!

I wondered how long it would take for her to get better. *Would* she really get better? Back to the way she had been?

As she walked, Mimi kept greeting people along the hall with her flashing smile. I love Mimi's smile, the one that used to greet me when I got off the bus after school. But looking at that bright face now, I just wanted to say, *Come on, Mimi! You're supposed to hate being in a place like this. So start hating it, and get better, and come home!*

I was happier when we got to Mimi's room, which was decorated with reminders of the *ranchita*. There was a big bouquet of yellow sunflowers from Mimi's garden. Her bright red *serape* was draped over a chair. One of her horse paintings hung on the wall, and taped up all around it were the wild, swirly ink drawings that Mimi had started to make with her left hand.

Mimi is right-handed, but after breaking her right wrist, she had started drawing with her left hand. Her new drawings were loose and free, full of mistakes yet so alive that they almost leaped off the wall.

New since yesterday was a drawing of Rembrandt, Mimi's black and white Border collie, who is currently living at my house with his brother Sam. Rembrandt's fur was made up of quick black squiggles. His eyes were inky blurs, but with that full-of-energy look that Border collies often get.

There were drawings of people, too—one of a nurse, drawn from the knees down, with thick calves and sensible shoes. *Is this lady thrilled to have her legs up there on the wall?* I wondered. Artists like Mimi don't tend to ask questions like that.

Mom, Mimi, and I sat and talked—well, Mom

talked, giving the same news she'd told Mimi yesterday. There isn't much new to tell somebody when you're visiting every day. Mimi just said "Mm-hmm" once in a while. She held her sketchpad in her right hand and scribbled with her left, looking up at me every few seconds. Her blue eyes were bright. She was having a fabulous time.

Me? Not so much. I *do* things with Mimi. We paint together, or we go for a ride. We talk about what's happening with the horses or on the canvas. I didn't know what to say to her right now, and she was too busy sketching to say much to me.

"Darn!" Mom said suddenly. "I left your mail in the car. I'll go get it."

As Mom left the room, Mimi turned the sketchpad so that I could see myself on the paper. My mouth turned down at the corners. My eyes were dark and shadowed.

"You don't look the happiest I've ever seen you," Mimi said gently.

I felt myself flush. "I just miss you," I said.

What a stupid thing to say! Mimi was sitting right there in front of me. How could I miss her?

But Mimi understood. "You miss our afternoons together," she said.

I waited for her to say, "Me too." That's what she was supposed to say. But she didn't. She sat there thinking for a minute.

"I'm learning a lot here," Mimi said finally. "I wouldn't recommend breaking two limbs just to get this opportunity, believe me! But it's jolted me out of my normal way of doing things, and in a way, that's exciting. Can you understand that?"

I could, actually. Mimi's left-handed drawings were cool, and nothing feels better than learning a new art technique or skill. Plus, Mimi was making friends here at the rehab center. I'd made a new friend myself recently in Gabi. I knew how fun that was. But it didn't make me feel any better right now. I'd been right: Mimi was having too good a time here. Where did that leave me?

"You were doing things differently already," I said. "Remember your pink horses?" That was the unfinished painting on Mimi's easel at the *ranchita*. She had drawn her herd of horses grouped close together. Their ears, necks, backs, and rumps made one continuous line. But the horses weren't painted with normal horse colors. They were watermelon-pink, the color of the Sandia Mountains at sunset.

Mimi had never done anything like that

painting before. And she'd forgotten all about it,
I could tell. When I mentioned the painting, Mimi's
face got all faraway and excited looking.

"You're right!" she said. "I'd love to get back to
that painting." She looked down at the cast on her arm.
"But for that, I need my right hand!" She sounded frustrated. Hurray! That was how I wanted her—frustrated
and determined, determined to get back home. I gave
her an encouraging thumbs-up.

"I *will* be back, Saige," Mimi said. "I promise
you that. Meantime, do some new things yourself!
You don't need to come here every day. Go paint.
Have something to show me when I get back. And
ride Picasso. You got him in shape for the parade at
the fiesta. It's not fair to just quit riding him now."

I felt a flutter of pride at the mention of the
parade, which I had led on majestic Picasso, Mimi's
oldest horse. Gabi and I had taught him to do some
tricks for the art fiesta, too, an act that we called the
Professor Picasso Show.

"Gabi has been coming to the *ranchita* with
me lately," I reminded Mimi. "I can't just ride off on
Picasso and leave her behind."

And if I paint, she'll want to paint, too, I thought
but didn't say. I was afraid to invite Gabi into Mimi's

studio. It was my special place, a place I'd shared only with Mimi—and sometimes Tessa, my best friend since kindergarten. I'd need to set up a canvas for Gabi, which would mean moving Mimi's half-finished painting aside—and I just couldn't bring myself to do that. I didn't want to change anything in the studio, at least not until Mimi could walk back into it with me.

"Hmm," Mimi said thoughtfully. "Maybe you two can ride together. Gabi can take Picasso, and you can start riding Georgia."

"*Georgia?*" I said in disbelief. Georgia was young, still in training. "Is she ready?"

"You're *both* ready," Mimi said. "I've watched you on Picasso. You've got a good seat and light hands, and you pay attention. And Georgia was getting to be steady and responsible—the last I saw of her, that is! I'll ask Luis to put you on a lunge line first. He'll be able to tell if this is a good idea. If you all feel comfortable, he can ride with you."

"Are you sure he has time?" I asked. Luis is Mimi's neighbor and good friend, but he's also a busy artist.

"Luis loves riding," Mimi said. "He used to be a cowboy, did you know that? He always says he spends too much time in his studio, and he's right.

He'll ride with you. Just ask him."

I smiled at Mimi's certainty. What could any of us say? One thing had not changed: Mimi gave the orders, and we obeyed.

And this was an order I *wanted* to obey. Go riding with my friend—what was there not to like about that?

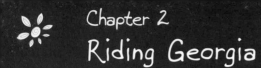

The next morning, Gabi and I walked the dogs before breakfast. It was mid-September now and cooler. The cottonwood trees in the backyards were turning yellow, and the scent of piñon smoke drifted out of someone's chimney and perfumed the air.

Overhead, two hot-air balloons—one yellow and one striped red, white, and blue—punctuated the clear blue sky. The neighborhood dogs barked at them. Not Sam and Rembrandt, though. Dad has a balloon, and both dogs have seen it launch a million times.

I explained Mimi's horseback-riding plan to Gabi. "I still don't know if it will happen," I added. "It depends on if Luis has time today."

"I bet he will," Gabi said.

"So can you come out with me this afternoon?" I asked. "Wear jeans and boots to school, just in case!"

"And if we don't ride, maybe we can paint in the studio," Gabi suggested hesitantly.

I felt my face turn red with shame. How could I not let Gabi paint with me in Mimi's studio? We *so* needed that after-school art program! Then Gabi would have art again, and I wouldn't have to invite her into my special place—the place I shared with Mimi.

I bent to pat Sam, hiding my face and avoiding a direct answer. "I bet you're right," I said to Gabi. "Luis will ride with us."

Half an hour later I met Gabi on the sidewalk. We both wore jeans and cowboy boots. I *love* my boots. You wouldn't think so to look at them, but they're actually really comfortable, and wearing them reminds me of being on Mimi's *ranchita*.

At school, we met Tessa and Dylan, who were already sitting at our table in Mrs. Applegate's fourth-grade classroom. Dylan glanced from Gabi's boots to mine and said, "Is it Dress Like a Cowboy Day? You should have called us!"

The back of my neck prickled, the way it sometimes does when I'm angry. Tessa went to music camp with Dylan this past summer, and since then, Dylan has been hanging out with us—*a lot*. I try to be nice to Dylan, but sometimes she really bugs me.

Luckily, Tessa's still Tessa, the friend who knows me best. While she and I were standing by the pencil sharpener, I told Tessa about my plan to go riding with Gabi today. "I hope Luis can ride with us," I said, "because if not, Gabi wants to paint in Mimi's studio, and I don't want that."

Suddenly Tessa looked a lot more interested—almost too interested. "Why not?" she asked, her eyes wide.

I tried to explain. "It was different having you there," I said. "You're *you*. You always used to come. But I don't want to change things in the studio. I'd have to take Mimi's painting off her easel, and . . ." My voice went husky. Was I going to cry? I pushed myself to say, "I—I want to try painting by myself. You got me through my painter's block, and I want to see what happens next."

Tessa nodded. "You're an artist," she said, her voice low and serious. "You have to pay attention to those things."

It felt good to be understood. Tessa's an artist, too—a singer and a musician. She knows what it's like to work at your art. And she believes that to get good at something, you have to practice for ten thousand hours. I was falling way, way behind on that.

"You should tell Gabi how you feel," Tessa said. "She'll understand, won't she?"

I shrugged. I wasn't sure Gabi *would* understand. I didn't want to bring the whole thing up, not if I didn't have to. "Maybe Luis will ride with us and none of this will matter," I said.

12

"No, you *have* to *tell* her," Tessa insisted.
"Artists have to be serious about these things. You
need to keep some time for yourself, and your friends
need to understand that."

I nodded, but I knew I couldn't say something
like that to Gabi. Tessa had hurt my feelings earlier
this fall when she'd started spending less time with
me and more with her music. I knew how that felt.
Why should I hurt Gabi's feelings if I didn't have to?

Luis and Carmen were both at the *ranchita*
when Gabi and I got off the bus. They're Mimi's closest
neighbors and good friends to our whole family. They
keep an eye on me and Gabi now that we spend time
at the *ranchita* without Mimi.

Luis is a silversmith and a blacksmith, and he
also does Spanish tinwork, an art form that dates back
to the early Spanish settlers. Luis is descended from
them, and Carmen is part Navajo. She's a quilter, a
weaver, and an incredible baker. I love spending time
with Luis and Carmen, and I especially love Carmen's
biscochitos, which she was just pulling out of the oven
when we arrived. Yum!

I sat down next to Gabi at Mimi's kitchen table

and reached for a warm cookie. Mimi's kitten was thrilled to have us there. Luis and Carmen had been looking in on her every day, but she was probably still missing Mimi—and even Rembrandt. She walked from my lap to Gabi's, purring loudly, her fluffy tail raised like a flag above the edge of the table.

We washed down our *biscochitos* with cold lemonade, and then—while Gabi and Carmen washed the glasses—I peeked through the studio doorway. The pink horses waited on Mimi's easel, fresh and full of promise. My easel stood empty. I was dying to take out a canvas and get started on something, but when Gabi stepped into the hallway, I turned away, as if I wasn't interested.

"Time to saddle up," Luis said. He, Gabi, and I filed through the front door and started for the barn. Carmen headed for Mimi's garden. She's been harvesting the tomatoes, peppers, squash, and gourds for Mimi. A part of me felt as if I should go help her, but I didn't—I'd been ordered to go for a ride, after all!

Mimi's horses are Spanish Barbs, a very old strain of horse that came over from Spain with the *conquistadores* more than four hundred years ago. In America, the Barbs helped the Indians hunt buffalo and the cowboys herd cattle. But Mimi told me that over time, the number of Spanish Barbs dropped, and they almost went extinct before some ranchers started to breed them again.

There still aren't many Spanish Barbs in this country—fewer than a thousand. That's why Mimi had five horses right now. She wants to do all she can to preserve the breed.

Gabi was excited about getting to ride Picasso. "I've never ridden a Barb before!" she told me. "Only Quarter Horses."

Gabi and I groomed Picasso together, and he seemed to love every minute of it. When Gabi's brush passed over one of his itchy spots, he nodded his head, the way we'd taught him to do for the Professor Picasso Show.

"He's clicking me!" Gabi said delightedly.
"I just did something *he* likes, so he's doing something *I* like, to say thank you."

"Picasso, you're so smart!" I said, hugging his neck.

We saddled Picasso, and Luis led him out to the ring, where Gabi mounted him. We watched her ride around the ring a few times at a walk, jog, and lope.

"You ride like a cowboy!" Luis said, giving

Gabi a thumbs-up. That made sense—I knew Gabi had learned to ride at her aunt and uncle's ranch. Watching her now, I felt a pinch of jealousy that she was riding my favorite horse. He was so beautiful! But then I thought of Georgia.

Georgia is a slender young mare, a rich red-brown with a black mane and tail. As I approached her in the barn, she looked surprised to see me. She arched her neck and sniffed me thoughtfully, her breath fluttering my hair. As I groomed her, she kept turning to look at me, shifting away from the brush. It made me a little uneasy about riding her.

"She's sensitive," Luis said from over my shoulder. It was as if he'd read my mind. "You just have to be very gentle."

Luis brought out a saddle and cinched it carefully beneath Georgia's belly. "See how I do this with her?" he said. "I barely tighten the girth at first. I let her take a few breaths to get used to it. Then I tighten it another notch and put on her bridle. Now I tighten the girth one more time and give her a nice scratch on the shoulder for being such a good girl."

Luis fastened a long horsehair rope to Georgia's bridle and then led her out to the ring, where Picasso and Gabi were still circling. When

I started to get on Georgia's back, she curved her neck around and sniffed me again, as if she'd never seen me before. I mounted slowly and carefully.

Luis adjusted my stirrups and backed up to the center of the ring, feeding out the long rope. "Ask her to walk," he said.

I squeezed gently with my legs. Georgia didn't move.

Luis said, "Ask again."

I did. Georgia lifted her head, put her ears back, and stood stock-still.

"Is she being stubborn?" I asked.

Luis said, "No. She's not sure what you want, so she's playing it safe and doing nothing. Sit tight, Saige. I'm going to swing the rope and send her forward. She may jump a little."

Uh-oh! I wrapped my free hand around the saddle horn. Luis gently swung the rope, but it came nowhere near Georgia. It wasn't meant to—it was just a signal. After a second, reluctantly, she took a step.

Yes! I wished I had a clicker and some carrot chunks to reward Georgia. Gabi and I had used clicker training to teach Picasso tricks for the Professor Picasso Show. It's a great way of explaining to an animal what you want him or her to do.

I didn't have a clicker, but I had plenty of praise for Georgia. "Good girl!" I told her enthusiastically. I felt her relax slightly beneath me. Now she understood that she'd done the right thing.

Georgia walked in a circle around Luis. Her ears turned constantly—toward him, straight ahead, and then toward the other end of the ring, where Gabi and Picasso stood and watched. But mostly her ears flicked back at me, over and over. I could almost hear her wondering, *Why are you up there? You mean other people can ride me, too?* The only person who'd ever ridden Georgia before was Mimi.

"She's a thinker, this one," Luis said. "Like Picasso at her age."

After a while, Luis had me nudge Georgia into a jog, and then a lope. I was surprised to feel Georgia's bumpy, choppy stride. She felt almost clumsy beneath me.

"How come she isn't smooth, like Picasso?" I asked.

"She's young," Luis said. "She doesn't know how to carry a rider yet, and she's not relaxed with you. She hasn't built up the muscle, either. That comes with time—time and work."

Time. I had time, long afternoons without Mimi

and without painting. Maybe for once, time was on my side.

After a while, Georgia seemed to decide that my riding her was okay. Her ears settled to a gentle, thoughtful angle, and she started responding better to my legs and reins.

Luis called me to the side of the ring to take off the lunge line. "Let's try riding her around the ring without it," he suggested. "She's pretty calm now, and being near Picasso will make her even calmer."

So Georgia and I slowly circled the ring, sometimes ahead of Gabi and Picasso, sometimes behind. For a while, we rode side by side.

"You both look much more relaxed," Gabi said.

I reached down and patted Georgia's neck. I was definitely starting to feel more relaxed, though not as relaxed as I am on Picasso.

"Excellent!" Luis called to us after a few more minutes. "Tomorrow maybe we'll ride together, all three of us."

Gabi nodded enthusiastically, but then paused and frowned. "Wait, I can't," she said. "Tomorrow my mom is taking me down to see Renata." Renata is Gabi's best friend from her old school in South Albuquerque.

Gabi seemed disappointed that she couldn't ride with us again, and I felt a little let down, too. Riding with Gabi was fun. But then I realized that with Gabi gone tomorrow, I could *paint*.

"Maybe Thursday then," Luis said. "Do you want to ride tomorrow, Saige?"

"No," I said quickly—too quickly. "I . . . I'll just . . . do something in the studio," I stammered. Gabi gave me a quick glance, and I wished I'd kept my mouth shut. But the truth was, I couldn't wait for tomorrow. It would feel so good to be back in front of my easel!

Wednesday afternoon when I got off the bus, I called Carmen and Luis, the way I was supposed to. I gathered eggs, fed and watered the chickens, and filled the horses' water tub. I waved to Carmen, who was now out working in Mimi's garden. Then I went into the studio.

The magical quiet slowly settled over me, a peace that I could find only in this special place. It amazed me that Mimi could draw at the rehab facility with people all around her. I needed quiet and privacy to find my way into that art space in my head.

I pinned up a reference picture on my easel. It was a newspaper photo of me leading the fund-raiser parade on Picasso. I'm not good at painting people's faces yet, so I zeroed in on Picasso's arched neck and beautiful head. I lightly sketched that image onto the canvas. Then I squeezed some paint onto my palette.

I brushed in the dark of Picasso's eyes, leaving a bar of white for his eyelashes. Time to move on from that part of the picture now, till the paint dried. I focused on the background, using dusky gray and purple—

Meep! Mimi's kitten jumped up onto my shoulder and hung on tight. My brush wavered. I put my left hand under my elbow to steady myself, adding more big sweeps of purple to the canvas.

Suddenly claws dug into my shoulder as the kitten sat and scratched her ear with her hind foot. A cloud of cat hairs drifted toward my glistening paint, tumbling and turning in the sunlight. They moved so slowly, it seemed as if I had plenty of time to grab them. But you can't grab floating cat hairs. When I reached for them, they swooped toward the canvas— as if the fresh paint were sucking them in. They were part of the picture now. If I tried to pick them off, I'd make an even worse mess.

"Ca-a-a-at!" I squawked, turning to look at the kitten, nose to nose. She stared back, eyes slightly crossing, and purred.

"Oh, never mind," I finally said. "How can I stay mad at you?" I gave her a kiss on the nose. But when I glanced back at the hairy purple background of my Picasso portrait, I groaned.

The kitten purred even louder. I cuddled her and took a step backward to give my painting a critical look.

Other than the layer of cat hair, the painting seemed familiar—too familiar. It was a lot like the picture I'd sold at the silent auction last weekend. Okay, Picasso's pose was different, his expression was different, and the background was different, but somehow the painting still felt like a copy. Happily and busily, I'd made the same choices I had made the last time I set up a painting. If Mimi had been at the next easel, she would have asked a question or two, and I might have had a fresh idea. Instead, I had just hit Rewind and Play again.

The kitten leaped off my shoulder. More cat hair twisted through the air toward the fresh paint. There was lots of texture there now. Hmm . . . maybe I could play with that.

By the time Dad arrived, I'd created a dark thicket of purplish thorns behind Picasso. I used the *impasto* method, which means laying paint on with a palette knife—a little tool that looks like the trowel Carmen was using out in the garden. You basically blob paint on with it and squish it around. The thick paint hid the hair and created a lot of texture.

The Picasso part of the painting was still a mostly blank canvas, but I liked how he looked, all pearly and mysterious. This was turning into a moody picture, almost like a fantasy. And all by accident!

Thursday afternoon Gabi came out to Mimi's with me, and Luis saddled up Frida so that he could ride with us in the pasture.

Frida is the mother of a lot of Mimi's horses—older, well-trained, and bossy. When I ride her and I don't do things just right, she *sighs*. It's an extremely disgusted sound, and it always makes me feel stupid.

Luis saddled Frida and took her for a couple of turns around the ring so that she could get used to him riding her. Frida never sighed once—Luis must have done everything right.

After Gabi and I were saddled up, too, we followed Luis and Frida into the back pasture. "We'll ride a bit in here first," Luis told us. "I want to see how Georgia does. If everything seems good, we'll go out into the *Bosque*."

The idea that everything might *not* seem good made me nervous, but Georgia paid no attention to my jitters. With the older horses near her, she seemed perfectly relaxed.

After ten minutes of riding in the pasture, Luis led us out the back gate into the *Bosque,* which means "woods" in Spanish. In this *bosque,* a belt of greenery along the Rio Grande, the trees are tall and airy. Light slides in under them onto the wispy undergrowth.

Today I noticed that the leaves were turning golden-green. Gabi and I tried to decide what color it was exactly—not lime-green or pistachio, not really chartreuse, and not really yellow either.

"There needs to be a crayon in the box called Autumn Cottonwoods," Gabi said.

"There needs to be a whole different *box* for New Mexico!" I said. "With hardly any greens, and lots of different browns. And Sandia Pink—"

"And Balloon Silk Yellow," Gabi added.

While we chattered about crayons, Luis hummed and then started singing softly. He loves *corridos*, Mexican ballads about outlaws and bandits. In real life you wouldn't want to meet those guys, but the songs sure are great.

When Luis started a song that Gabi and I knew, we joined in. At the sound of my voice, Georgia's ears swiveled curiously. Luis interrupted his singing to say, "Georgia likes the sound of your voice. Mimi sings to the young horses when she rides. It calms them down."

I was relieved that somebody actually liked my singing. I hadn't sung since a few weeks ago, when Tessa had told me I was off-key. Even in music class, I faked it. But Georgia was happy, and Gabi

25

didn't seem to have a problem with how I sang. Neither did Luis. Frida didn't even sigh, which says a lot!

Luis made his voice soft and sweet, and I tried to follow along, more confidently with each verse. Gabi and I grinned at each other as we sang, the horses stepping slowly through the beautiful *Bosque*.

Halfway through our third or fourth song, all three horses stopped in their tracks, pointing their ears hard at a place where the brush rustled and shifted. I looked over at Luis. He was staring as intently as the horses. "Coyote," he whispered, and then I saw it, melting away from us through the brush.

Georgia had been standing still as a statue. Now she bobbed her head and took a step after the coyote. Luis laughed. "Oh, you're one of those!" he said. "She wants to follow that coyote, Saige. She has courage, which is natural for Spanish Barbs. And they love to herd other animals. Let her take a few steps— that's fine. Now take up your rein a little. That tells her, 'No, you're with me.'"

I did as Luis told me to do. Georgia's ears looked disappointed, but eventually she relaxed and moved along with the others.

We'd come a long way by now. Luis turned us around, and we headed back toward the *ranchita*

while he told us stories about his cowboy days. "We used to train young horses by riding them at the tail end of a moving herd," he said. "By the time we got to where we were going, the horses were pretty confident about driving cattle."

Luis grinned and glanced over at Georgia. "I doubt this one would need that much training, though," he added, reaching over to pat her neck. I could tell he thought Georgia was pretty special, and I did, too.

I smiled at Gabi, who was enjoying every moment on Picasso. She liked so many of the same things I did. She'd become a great friend—maybe even as good a friend as Tessa.

By the time we'd gotten back to the *ranchita*, I'd made a decision. After we put the horses away, I said to Gabi, "Come into the studio. I want to see what my painting looks like today."

Gabi didn't say anything, but she looked pleased. She nodded and followed me toward Mimi's house.

I opened the studio door and looked at my painting with a fresh eye. The impasto background was really working! And the unpainted shape of Picasso made me long to pick up a brush and fill it in.

Gabi walked around the studio, hands in her pockets. She looked at everything as if she was really interested, but she didn't say a word.

I was feeling so relaxed that I did something that surprised even me: I asked Gabi, "Do you . . . want to paint with me tomorrow?"

Gabi opened her mouth to respond with what I thought would be a big "YES," but then I saw her expression change. "Umm . . . no, that's okay," she said with a little smile. "But thanks."

I was stunned. All along, I'd thought Gabi wanted nothing more than to come and paint with me in Mimi's studio. So why did she say no?

At school the next day, Tessa made sure we got some alone time at the computer. "I told Gabi yesterday," she said in a low voice.

"Told her what?" I asked. I had no idea what Tessa was talking about.

"I told her about how you need time to do your art," Tessa said. "I mean, I didn't tell her straight out, because I knew you didn't want to, but I dropped some big hints."

I was shocked. "What *kind* of hints?" I asked.

Tessa cocked her head, recalling her words. "I told her . . ." she began. "I said, 'Saige needs to be alone to do her work' and 'Artists really need space from their friends.' Stuff like that."

Well, *that* explained Gabi's response in the studio yesterday. I didn't know what to say to Tessa, who seemed so pleased with herself. Maybe I did work better in the studio when I was alone. I had started a painting, after all. But that was for *me* to decide, not Tessa. She never should have gone behind my back and told Gabi about it.

I almost snapped at Tessa and told her to butt out, but I didn't. Tessa had obviously hurt Gabi's feelings, but that didn't mean I had to hurt *Tessa's* feelings, too. For a second I thought wistfully of the good old days, when I'd had only one close friend. Life had been a lot less complicated then!

I didn't get the chance to straighten things out with Gabi. She seemed focused on her schoolwork all day, and afterward, I had to hurry out front. Mom was picking me up to go see Mimi.

When we got to the rehab center, Mimi was talking with an old lady in a wheelchair. She had expressive white eyebrows and amazing wrinkles, and there was something sweet about the way she smiled, like she'd spent a lifetime expecting good things. She made Mimi look young and strong, and I liked that.

"Oh, good!" Mimi said when she saw us. She introduced us to the lady, Agnes Fane.

"Isn't that your teacher's—" Mom started to ask, when in walked Miss Fane herself, my art teacher from last year. My favorite teacher of all time! I was relieved to see that she hadn't changed a bit—her blonde hair was still cut in a curly bob, and she was all smiles, like her aunt Agnes. Miss Fane seemed as surprised to see me as I was to see her, and very impressed to meet Mimi.

Miss Fane had flowers and a vase in her hands. "Can you show me where the ladies' room is, Saige?" she asked. "I want to get these in water."

As we walked, she explained that her aunt Agnes had fallen and broken her hip—a much worse injury than Mimi's. She was very old, and her bones were fragile.

"What about your grandmother?" Miss Fane asked. "Did she fall off a horse? I've read that she's quite the rider." Mimi is semi-famous, at least in Albuquerque. She has exhibits at galleries, and newspapers sometimes write articles about her.

"She tripped over Rembrandt," I said.

"Rembrandt the dog, that is."

Miss Fane laughed. "Oh, that's funny!" she said. "I mean—not *funny*, but what a great thing to be able to say!"

I laughed, too. That's what I love about Miss Fane. She's so easy to be with. I explained Mimi's accident while Miss Fane filled the vase with water. She plumped up the bouquet so that it looked pretty, and we took it back to the commons room. Mom, Mimi, and Aunt Agnes were gabbing away, as if they'd known one another forever.

"Let's not interrupt," Miss Fane said. "Shall we take a walk? Tell me what you've been doing lately. Drawing and painting, I hope?"

As we wandered along the halls, I told Miss Fane about my painting for the silent auction and about the one I was doing now, complete with cat hairs. "I really miss art in school, though," I said. "We've raised money for an after-school class, but it hasn't started yet. I never thought it would be so complicated!"

Miss Fane sighed. "I hope you can get the class going," she said. "Kids who have art in school do better academically. That's not the only reason you should have art, but it ought to motivate the powers that be!"

The Discovery

As we walked on, Miss Fane talked about what she was teaching the kids at her other school. This was the part of the year, leading up to Balloon Fiesta, when she taught about the color wheel and had kids design their own balloons. Not *fair*!

"I wish we were doing that," I said longingly, and then I got a great idea. "Hey, our school needs an art teacher to lead the after-school classes. Would you . . . ?"

Miss Fane smiled wryly and shook her head. "I wish I could," she said, "but I'm teaching full-time and looking after things for Aunt Agnes. I couldn't do it. But I'll put the word out with other artists and teachers I know."

I turned away to hide my disappointment. I missed Miss Fane *so* much! I struggled to think of something else to say—a way to change the subject—and that's when I saw it: a closed door at the end of the hallway with a placard on the wall. In white letters it read "Art Room."

Miss Fane and I glanced at each other. I raised my eyebrows as if to say, *Should we peek?*

"Try the door," Miss Fane urged. She seemed as excited about this discovery as I was.

I twisted the door handle, expecting it to be

locked. But the door opened. We stepped into the room, and Miss Fane flipped the light switch.

This was a large room, and clearly it wasn't used anymore. Tables and chairs were crammed into the center of the floor. I saw several easels at the back of the room, standing around like a flock of sandhill cranes. There was a loom holding a half-finished rug, a row of unglazed pots, and jars of beads. The large plastic bins lining the shelves were labeled "Drawing," "Paints and Brushes," "Paper," and "Canvas."

I ran my finger along a shelf, making a trail in the dust. Nothing here had been touched in a while.

"I *thought* there used to be an art program here," Miss Fane said. "Lots of hospitals and rehab centers have them. They really help patients heal faster. It makes sense, doesn't it? Art makes you feel better. But it tends to be the first thing cut when budgets get tight."

"Just like at school," I murmured, and then I said, "I have to show Mimi!"

We hurried back to the commons room. Miss Fane sat down beside her aunt, and I said, "Mimi, come see! We just found something amazing!"

"How far away is this amazing thing?" Mom asked. "Can Mimi walk that far?"

The Discovery

"It's good for me to walk," Mimi said. "But bring the chair, in case I poop out."

We made a slow parade down the hall, Mimi clip-clopping with her walker, Mom pushing the empty wheelchair, and me dancing around in front of them, then dashing ahead to make sure I was taking them in the right direction. It's easy to get lost in a place like this, but I remembered right and found the room. I opened the art room door and turned to Mimi.

"Look!" I declared, pointing out the easels, the bins of supplies, and the floor still streaked with paint and dried clay. "What do you think? Could we paint here when I come visit?"

Mimi looked around, bright-eyed. "I don't see why not," she said after a moment. "At least, it won't hurt to ask the director. If we hurry, we might be able to catch her in her office. Steady that chair for me, please." Mimi eased herself gently into the wheelchair and then grinned up at me. "Step on it, driver!"

That made me giggle. It sounded like the old Mimi that I know and love. As I took off with her down the hall, Mom followed with the walker, urging caution. But Mimi was in charge, as usual, and we powered down the hallways at a fast clip.

We caught the director just as she was locking up her office, and we learned that Miss Fane was right: There *had* been an art therapy program here until budget cuts closed it down. The director was trying to get it up and running again.

"And I will," she said in a firm voice. "It's so valuable for people recovering from illness and trauma. Meanwhile, yes—if you can clear some space, Saige, you and Mimi are welcome to paint there."

"May we use the easels and paints?" Mimi asked. "It would be easier than bringing them from home."

"Certainly," the director said. "Feel free to use what you need." She must have known that Mimi is an artist. Sometimes it's useful to have a famous grandmother!

That night, a knock on the door told me that Gabi was here, ready to help me walk the dogs. My dog, Sam, and Mimi's dog, Rembrandt, like each other better now, and I can walk them by myself. But Gabi loves dogs and doesn't have one. Her dog died just before they moved here, and her mother is waiting till they are settled in before getting a new one. Since

The Discovery

I have an "extra" dog for now, we're sharing.

While we walked, Gabi seemed shy, the way she had before we really knew each other. She wouldn't look me in the eye. *Oh, Tessa!* I thought. I had to fix this.

"Hey," I said. "What Tessa said about me needing time alone to do my art—don't worry about it, okay?"

Gabi looked startled. I knew she hadn't expected me to bring this up.

"It was because of something I told her, but it isn't really true," I said. I tried to explain to Gabi how I felt about Mimi's studio, how I didn't want to change things there. "I know it's crazy—"

"No," Gabi interrupted, "I get it. I mean"—she used her free hand, the one not holding a leash, to gesture toward the houses on the street—"we just moved. I don't even know where I am half the time when I wake up in the morning. I *love* places that stay the same!"

I felt stunned. I'd never thought about that. "Poor Gabi!" I said, reaching over to put my hand on her shoulder. "I'm sorry."

Now I wanted more than ever to invite Gabi to paint in Mimi's studio with me. I opened my mouth to ask when I suddenly remembered the room I'd discovered at the rehab center. "Hey, guess what I found today?" I said. I told Gabi about the art room and how Dad and I were going to move things around to make space for Mimi and me to work. "Do you want to help?" I asked. "Maybe we could even ask the director if you can come paint with us."

"With you and Mimi?" Gabi asked. "Wow!" Her smile was all the answer I needed.

At that moment, a huge weight seemed to lift off my shoulders. I'd been ready to share Mimi's studio, but now I didn't have to. Gabi, Mimi, and I would finally get some art time, in a new room that we could create *together*.

Sunday afternoon, Dad, Gabi, and I spent about an hour moving things around in the art room. Mimi watched from the corner, with lots of opinions about how we could do things better. "Lift with your knees, not your back," she suggested, and "Wouldn't you get more light if you set those up at the other end of the room?" I could tell she wished she could get up out of her chair and do all of this herself.

We found plenty of acrylic paints in the plastic bins. Some had dried up, but others were still okay. We found brushes and palettes, too, but no prepared canvases.

"Why don't you bring some from my studio, Saige," said Mimi. "There's a stash in a box behind the couch. And bring my thumb palette, too. I think that would be easiest for me to work with." Mimi paused to take a breath and reached over to squeeze my hand. "Oh, I'm excited about this! Aren't you?"

I was *way* more than excited. Mimi was finally focused on her art again. I couldn't wait for tomorrow afternoon!

That night I ate supper at Gabi's house. Mr. Peña was away at a conference, so it was just going to be her mom and us kids. "Let's talk about dogs *a lot* tonight," Gabi told me as we went up their walk. "I'm afraid my mom's forgetting her promise."

Mrs. Peña had promised that Gabi could get a dog once the family was settled in their new home. But as I walked through the front door, I noticed that *nothing* looked settled yet. There was still a huge box in the living room. Roberto, Gabi's four-year-old brother, had colored on it and surrounded it with toys. A rug was rolled up in one corner of the room, and a bunch of knickknacks were squashed together on the top of what was otherwise an empty bookshelf. The house didn't seem ready for a preschooler, let alone a dog.

But I did what Gabi wanted. While Mrs. Peña finished cooking supper, we talked about dogs—dogs in general, dogs we'd seen on the street, the way the neighborhood dogs bark at hot-air balloons, and of course, Sam and Rembrandt.

"They like each other so much these days," I said. "That's because of Gabi's training. She's really amazing with dogs."

"Sam and Rembrandt are great," Gabi said. "But you know, if you need a break, one of them could stay overnight here. I really miss—"

Mrs. Peña turned from the stove, with Gabi's baby sister balanced on one hip and a dripping spoon in her other hand. Mrs. Peña was smiling, but she also looked a little annoyed.

"Gabi," she said pointedly, "I may be a tired mother and a busy mother, but I am not a stupid mother. You girls don't need to keep talking about dogs. The plan, Gabi, is this: On your birthday, we'll go to the shelter and see if we can find the right dog for our family. But *until* that day, you need to be patient and stop reminding me. Does that sound like a good plan?"

As her mom talked, Gabi's face flushed pink with excitement. She didn't say anything, but she grabbed a pen and raced to the calendar. She flipped the pages to December, and on December third, she scribbled a joyous five-pointed star.

"When's your birthday, Saige?" Gabi asked, turning around with her pen poised.

"October eighth," I said.

"Oh!" Gabi said. "Right in the middle of Balloon Fiesta! What do you do for your birthday? I mean, your dad's a balloon pilot, right? So he's probably really into the Fiesta. How do you have time for a birthday?"

"No, it's fun," I explained to her. "It's like a nine-day birthday party! We have a little family party, just us and Mimi, at Dad's balloon during a Glow." Glows are when the pilots light up their balloons at night. They're tethered, so they stay on the ground. Balloon Fiesta Park is filled with gigantic, glowing shapes, like the biggest birthday cake in the world.

I went on. "And one night during Fiesta," I said, "Tessa sleeps over, and we get up really early and go up in the balloon with Dad, all by ourselves."

Gabi's eyes lit up. "Cool," she said under her breath. The expression on her face read, *I'd like to do that, too.* She didn't say anything out loud, but I was getting good at hearing what Gabi *wasn't* saying. I liked that. It showed that we were meant to be friends.

Gabi turned back to the calendar and marked a big star on my birthday. But now, I realized, my birthday was getting complicated.

Dad's balloon isn't huge. It can carry only three adults. We're kids and small, so probably Tessa and Gabi could both come. But what would Tessa think about that? And what about Dylan? If I had Gabi with me, Tessa might want Dylan with her. That's *definitely* too many people.

Aargh! Maybe I should hold a raffle!

Monday morning when we all gathered at our classroom table, I told Tessa and Dylan about the abandoned art room. "I'm really glad I found it," I said boldly, making sure Tessa was listening, "because I couldn't ask *anybody* to paint at Mimi's studio without changing things there, and I didn't want to do that."

Tessa looked from me to Gabi. "Ohhh," she said slowly, as if to say, *You told her how you felt?*

I smiled and gave Tessa a knowing look, a look that I hoped would say, *Yes, Gabi knows. Now there's no more secret.*

Dylan picked up on our silent signals. "What's going on?" she asked, narrowing her eyes.

I wanted to give *her* a look that said, *It's none of your business,* but I didn't. I just kept talking about the art room until my friends seemed as excited about it as I was.

That afternoon I walked into the rehab facility art room with canvases under my arm and smocks draped over my shoulder. Mimi was waiting for me.

It was just the two of us today, trying out the art room for the first time. But I hoped Gabi would be able to come tomorrow.

I put the canvases on our easels, helped Mimi get the smock on over her broken wrist, and opened the paint tubes. That's hard to do one-handed. Then I settled in at my own easel, ready to start.

I was a little distracted at first, watching Mimi figure out how to paint with a broken wrist. She's so skillful with a brush, but all of that skill was trapped inside the plaster cast on her right hand.

"Maybe you could try impasto," I suggested, thinking of my cat-hair adventures.

"Good idea!" said Mimi. She put the thumb palette on her right hand and picked up a palette knife with her left. "Let's see if I can hit the canvas more often than I hit the floor," she joked. She sliced into a blob of paint and squished it onto the canvas. "Bull's-eye!"

Mimi's eyes sparkled. She seemed to be taking all of this change in stride. After all, she'd learned to draw with her left hand, so maybe she *would* get somewhere with the slice-and-squish method.

Okay, what was *I* going to paint? A horse, of course—

No, wait a minute! I already had a horse picture on the easel at Mimi's studio. I paused to let my mind drift, and then I remembered Miss Fane talking about having her students design balloons. I love balloons, and I know a lot about them. Maybe I could do a balloon painting.

I started sketching shapes onto the canvas with a charcoal pencil and thinking about colors. Blue, against a blue sky, would be a fun challenge. It would need a belt of red or orange . . .

After a few minutes, Mimi came over, her walker clanking across the floor. She was moving better this week, stronger and more sure of herself.

Mimi stood behind me and looked at my canvas. "That's going to be lovely," she said. "And I think your audience agrees."

I glanced over my shoulder at the doorway, where a few patients had gathered to watch us paint. "Mimi!" I whispered, suddenly wishing I could hide behind her.

"Nothing attracts attention like an artist at work," Mimi said calmly.

"But—"

"You're in a public space, my dear," Mimi said, "and art is a public activity. We *say* we do our art to please ourselves, but then we hang it on the wall, don't we?"

Mimi was right about that. And I certainly didn't mind when Miss Fane turned up a few minutes later. So, okay, I guess I had mixed feelings about an audience.

The facility director dropped by to see how things were going, too, and that gave me a chance to ask her if Gabi could paint with us. The director looked around at the patients, all so interested in watching us work. "I don't see why not," she said. "Especially since she helped whip this old room into shape."

So Tuesday afternoon I set up an easel for Gabi. I was getting her started with acrylics when Miss Fane came in with her aunt. I introduced Gabi to Miss Fane, and when Gabi began asking Miss Fane questions about how to get started on her painting, I went back to my own canvas. It felt just like art class—working away on my project and listening to Miss Fane teach.

At the end of the afternoon, Miss Fane looked wistfully at the rest of the easels, separated from us by a maze of stacked tables and chairs. "I don't suppose you thin young people could worm through and bring two more of those out?" she asked. "Aunt Agnes and I would love to paint with you."

"Sure!" I said.

"Can you bring three?" asked a man in a wheelchair who had been watching us paint all afternoon.

How could we say no? Gabi and I made our way back to the easels and brought out six more, just in case there were other people here who wanted to paint with us. Who knew how big this thing was going to get?

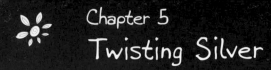

It got bigger. A lot bigger.

That week Gabi and I painted with Mimi every afternoon. I worked slowly and lovingly on my sky, trying to get it just right. Meanwhile the blank balloon shapes beckoned, and soon I was brushing in the colors. I felt as if I'd been hungry, and now I was getting to sit down to a big feast.

More people joined us every day. It was fun watching them work. The man in the wheelchair squinted and stuck out his tongue as he painted. One lady frowned and sighed. Aunt Agnes put delicate little dabs of color, pinks and lavenders and golds, onto her canvas. I couldn't tell what she was painting, but it looked pretty.

By Friday, all the artists seemed to be enjoying their work, but as I glanced around the room, I felt a sudden pang. The people here had gotten art just by accident. We kids had worked hard for an after-school class, and what did we have? Nothing yet.

Well, that wasn't quite true. Gabi and I could paint here, at least, and my balloons were getting better and better. Every time the balloons improved, I had to do more work on my sky. Usually, I love how that happens, how one change leads to another and the painting takes on a life of its own. But today, I felt fidgety and restless. Why did I suddenly feel so eager to finish this painting?

Suddenly I heard Mimi's voice behind me.

"Ah, Saige paints the sky," she murmured. "That picture is lovely, but it makes me feel sad, too."

I turned around, surprised. "Really?" I asked.

"It's a fine painting," Mimi reassured me. "But every time I see it, I want to get out of here! Go for a ride. Get up in a balloon with the wind in my hair."

That was why I felt edgy. "Me, too!" I said. I hadn't spent time outside in days—not since we'd started using the art room.

"Then go!" Mimi said. "You can be out there, up in your dad's balloon or riding Georgia. I can't—yet." She looked grumpy. "It's annoying. I wanted to have Georgia rock-solid by October."

The thought of beautiful young Georgia made me smile. I missed her! "But why October?" I asked Mimi.

"I was hoping to turn her over to a new owner by then," Mimi said, clumping back to her own canvas. "She needs someone who can give her the attention she deserves."

My stomach clenched at Mimi's words. *A new owner?*

Mimi selling Georgia shouldn't have been a shock. Preserving Spanish Barb horses is Mimi's mission. That means selling them so that lots of people get to know them, show them off, and care about them.

Georgia would become a wonderful riding horse. She had gotten steadier and smoother with every ride, and I'd felt proud about helping with that. But had I just been making her easier to sell?

I felt a lump form in my throat. *You've just gotten to know Georgia,* I reminded myself. It wasn't as if Mimi was selling Picasso, whom I'd known all my life. So why was I getting so upset about this?

"Maybe I'll go riding tomorrow," I said, trying to keep my voice light. "If Gabi or Luis wants to." I should grab as many rides on Georgia as possible, before it was too late.

"Do that," Mimi said. But as I turned back to my own easel, I couldn't lift my hand. The sparkle and creativity had left my brush.

Saturday morning Gabi and I went riding with Luis. It was hard to enjoy it at first. I didn't feel like singing, and I couldn't be happy about Georgia's good

manners or the way her stride had smoothed out.
Gabi noticed and asked me what was wrong.

"Mimi's going to sell Georgia," I said.

We were all riding side by side up the dirt road.
Luis, on the other side of Gabi, looked at me sharply.
"Is she?" he asked. "What makes you think that?"

I told him what Mimi had said. "She thinks
Georgia needs someone who can give her more
attention," I said glumly.

"I see," Luis said. "Well, Georgia has certainly
blossomed with attention from you. But don't worry,
Saige," he added, a warm smile in his eyes. "It's not so
easy to sell horses these days. It takes time."

"That's true," Gabi said earnestly. "My uncle
was just talking about that. He has all these good
horses for sale, and no buyers. So it probably won't
happen, at least not anytime soon."

I gave Gabi a grateful smile. Her words made
me feel better—but also kind of guilty, because if
nobody did buy Georgia, that might be bad for her,
and bad for Spanish Barbs. They're so rare. They
need people to love them, ride them, breed them, and
spread the word about them. I could do the first two
things—love Georgia and ride her. But I guess that
wasn't enough.

As if she sensed my feelings, Georgia tossed
her black mane and pricked her ears at the trail ahead,
dancing a little under me. *Cheer up!* she seemed to say.
We're here today. Life is good. I patted her sleek neck
and felt my spirits lift a little.

After our ride, Luis invited us over to visit
with Carmen. Their house is a small adobe, dark and
cool inside like Mimi's house. The walls are bright
with Carmen's quilts, and ornate tinwork sconces and
chandeliers hang everywhere. I also spotted racks full
of the earrings and bracelets Luis makes out of metal
and horsehair. He and Carmen were getting ready
for Balloon Fiesta, where they usually sell a lot of
their artwork. The Fiesta and Christmas are every
Albuquerque artist's busy season.

Gabi looked around, wide-eyed. "Tinwork is
so cool!" she said, waving her hand at the walls. "We
have some at home that my great-grandfather made.
I'd love to learn how to do it."

"Me, too!" I said. "Maybe you could teach us,
Luis."

I had a feeling Luis would be a great teacher.
Suddenly I flashed on my teacher Miss Fane, who

had been helping with the painting afternoons at the rehab center. I pictured all the patients there who had been painting side by side with me over the last week. "They'd all love it," I said aloud, and then had to explain to everyone what I was talking about.

"Hmm," Luis said. "I could probably go over there and teach a class or two. I'll talk with Mimi about it."

Gabi and I shared an excited glance. If Mimi got involved, the tinwork class was *sure* to happen!

It took Mimi only two days to get Luis scheduled to teach at the rehab center. Once Mimi was out of rehab, I'd have to put her to work on our after-school art class. Mimi knows how to get things done! And with any luck, trying to get the after-school class off the ground would distract her from selling Georgia.

Luis decided to teach jewelry making first. Hurray! I love jewelry, but the best part is, so does Tessa. Her eyes lit up when I told her about it, and she decided to come with me to Luis's class.

Tuesday afternoon, Luis called the class to order, and all of us—twelve patients, Miss Fane, and

we three girls—learned how to make rings and bracelets out of silverware. Luis buys old forks, knives, and
spoons at yard sales, so he brought a plastic bag full,
plus a small jewelry torch. He used the torch to heat
the silver, and with pliers and a clamp, helped each
person twist his or her piece into shape.

When my turn came, I shaped a silver butter
knife into a cool, wavy-shaped bracelet. Tessa made
a ring using rough, unpolished turquoise chips that
Luis had brought. "Turquoise is a charm for riders,"
he told us. "The old people say a rider wearing
turquoise will never be thrown and the horse will
never tire."

"*Oh!*" Gabi and I said together. When Luis rode
with us, he always wore turquoise on his hatband.

"We should wear turquoise, then," I said. But
when I saw Luis packing up his materials, I knew
there wasn't time to start another project. I couldn't
believe how quickly class had flown by.

"That was fun," Tessa said, admiring her new
ring. "When are they going to start our after-school
art classes, do you know? I'll probably come. I forgot
how much I like art."

Wow! I thought. I hadn't heard Tessa say a
good word about art in weeks. It had become such an

issue between us. This was big.

Before I could respond, I saw Mom peek into the doorway of the art room. She pointed at the wall clock. That meant it was time to head out and take care of chores at the *ranchita*.

I went to say good-bye to Mimi, who was chatting with Luis. "Oh, are you leaving?" she asked me. "Wait a minute and I'll walk you to the front door."

That seemed like a long walk to me. "Wow! Is that okay, Mimi?" I asked. "Are you supposed to do that?"

"As often as possible," Mimi said. "And it feels—*okay* is a good way to put it. But a little more okay every day." As we walked along together, I noticed that I was still faster than Mimi, but not that much faster. Time was passing. She was healing.

"It was nice having Tessa here today," Mimi said. "She seemed to be enjoying herself."

"She was," I agreed. "She asked about the after-school classes, too. But we *still* don't know when they'll start. We need to find a few good art teachers, I guess." I glanced down at my new silver bracelet. "Hey!" I said to Mimi. "How about Luis?"

Mimi shook her head and smiled. "No, Saige," she said quickly. "Luis has his hands full with the ranch, and he barely has enough time to do his own artwork, let alone teach it." When Mimi saw the look on my face, she added, "There are teachers out there. It'll all come together—you'll see."

"*When?*" I asked. My voice was loud, surprising even me. "At this rate, by the time after-school art gets going, half the year will be over!" I hadn't known all of those words were going to pour out. A nurse looked my way, startled.

"You're right," Mimi said gently, giving the nurse a look that said, *Don't worry, I've got this.* "You kids may need to remind everyone just how important art is to you."

You kids? I'd been hoping Mimi would swing into action herself. "But what can we do?" I asked, trying to keep my voice from rising again.

"I'm not sure," Mimi said. "Let's both give it some thought." We reached the front door. I held it open for Mimi, and she stepped out onto the front walk and looked across the parking lot, where Mom waited for me beside the car. The wind whisked up little dust devils. The shadows were long, and the sky was pale blue.

"Wish I were going with you to the *ranchita*," Mimi said. "If I could only go for a ride right now . . ."

She sighed. "That's where I've always gotten my best ideas—on the back of a horse."

She turned back toward the door. It was big and heavy, and I rushed to pull it open for her. *You'll be riding soon,* I wanted to say, but there was a big difference between walking down a hallway and hopping on a horse's back. I didn't want to say anything too unrealistic. Mimi tends to get annoyed at that.

Mom pulled up beside me and I got into the car, thinking back over what Mimi had just said. How were we kids going to remind people how much we cared about art? I wished an idea would drop out of the sky, but it didn't. Maybe, like Mimi, I would need to spend some time on horseback to figure things out.

The next morning before school, I met Gabi, Dylan, and Tessa at our table. I was wearing my bracelet, and Tessa was showing off the ring she'd made yesterday. "That was fun!" she told me again. "I can't wait for the after-school class to start. I'll definitely come."

"But when is it going to happen?" Dylan asked sharply. Of all of us, she was the only one who hadn't had any art all year. It looked as if that was bothering her.

"Mimi says we have to remind teachers and the principal how much we need art," I answered. "Does anybody know how we can do that?"

"Let's go on strike!" Dylan suggested. "*They* don't get homework till *we* get art."

"That's kind of negative," Gabi said, scrunching her brow. "I mean, we're all on the same side, right? Our teachers probably want more art in school, too."

"And art is good for us academically," I said, remembering what Miss Fane had told me. "If we have art, we'll do better in middle school and high school—and that will make *this* school look even better. Everybody should want that. We could make some charts or graphs and write a report full of interesting facts—"

"Blah, blah, blah," said Dylan scornfully. "Sorry, but a few facts will never get people to do anything."

"How do you know?" I asked. Dylan was bugging me. She's such a know-it-all!

"My mom talks about this stuff all the time," Dylan answered. "She's a newspaper reporter. She always says, 'Facts alone don't make people do things. It takes a good story to give facts power.' And a story is about somebody *doing* something. We have to *do* something!"

"Okay. But what?" I asked.

We all looked at one another, and after a moment, we all shrugged. *Great!* We were right back where we had started.

"Well, let's think," I said. "We should all try to come up with ideas tonight—"

"I know, I know!" Gabi broke in. "Before we go to sleep, we should ask ourselves what we can do. Maybe we'll dream the answer."

"Does that ever work?" Tessa asked, and then we all started interrupting one another to tell about interesting dreams we'd had.

But at the end of the day, I reminded my friends: *"Think!"*

A Solo Ride

Gabi couldn't come riding with me in the afternoon. Her mother had to take the little kids to a doctor's appointment, and she needed Gabi's help managing them. Gabi would be great at that, I thought. She'd probably have Roberto completely clicker-trained before the appointment was over.

When I got to the *ranchita,* I asked Luis, "Do you think I could ride Georgia by myself? I need to think, and she might help me do that."

Luis hesitated and then said, "How about this? I need to ride fence for Mimi—"

"Ride fence?" I asked. "What does that mean?"

Luis laughed. "That's cowboy talk," he said. "It means to ride around the fence line and make repairs. So let's do this. I'll ride out on Picasso and do what I need to do. You come with me and ride Georgia near us. It's a big pasture. I'll be able to see you, but you'll be able to ride Georgia and get some good thinking time, too." He winked at me.

"Okay!" I agreed. Mimi's horse pasture is huge. It seemed like a big adventure, riding Georgia without Luis right by my side.

We caught Picasso and Georgia and locked the

other horses into the corral. Then we saddled up.
Luis strapped a saddlebag full of tools behind his
saddle. He buckled a leather scabbard onto the saddle,
too. That was meant to hold a rifle, for hunting, but
Luis filled it up with fiberglass fence posts, white
poles about as thick around as a pencil. He started to
mount up, and then laughed and stepped back down
to unplug the electric fence. "That would have been
a big mistake!" he said, making a face at me. Then
we both mounted and rode through the gate into the
open pasture.

I felt like a cowboy, riding along the fence line
with Luis. His attention was on the fence, and so was
mine. We were working.

A little way out, the fence sagged. Luis
dismounted to tighten it. He dropped Picasso's reins,
and Picasso stood there, ground-tied. He wouldn't
move until Luis came back to him.

"I'll go on ahead," I said.

Luis nodded. "If she gets nervous, just circle
back toward us, okay?" he said.

I nodded and then urged Georgia on. A lot of
horses don't like to leave their friends, but Georgia
didn't hesitate. I rode her along the eastern fence line,
farthest from the *Bosque*. Georgia's stride was swift

and smooth. When I looked back, Luis and Picasso were small in the distance. I felt as if I was riding alone. Riding *Georgia* alone. For the first time ever. It was a big deal, but it also seemed simple and natural somehow.

After a few minutes, I asked Georgia to jog. A jog is the slow trot cowboys use when they're going to be riding all day. Georgia wanted to go faster. I said no with the reins, and she agreed. Her hooves drummed—one-two, one-two, one-two, one-two. It reminded me of the rhythm of some of the cowboy songs Luis and I sing.

That reminded me that I had a cowboy job to do. I started paying attention to the fence as I rode. Mimi uses electric tape fencing, the wide kind that looks like construction zone tape. It was old and had knots tied in it, but it seemed to be holding up. Luis wouldn't have to do anything here.

The world glided slowly past. I felt part of it, loose and free. Riding alone, I didn't have to talk. I could think my own thoughts, or not think at all. But I wasn't alone. I had Georgia.

For how much longer? I sensed Georgia thinking hard, too, and being careful, like a little girl trying hard to be responsible. She was so good and beautiful, she was bound to sell easily, no matter what Luis thought. If I knew as much about animal training as Gabi, I could teach her to be bad, and maybe she'd never sell—but I couldn't do that to her, and I couldn't do that to Mimi.

"I love you, Georgia," I said aloud. A dark ear tipped back at me.

Then both ears suddenly sharpened on something ahead—a gray-brown coyote trotting across the pasture.

Georgia stared after the coyote, tugging on the reins. She wanted to chase him. "No. Sorry, brave girl," I said, patting her neck. Mr. Coyote glanced over his shoulder and took off like a shot. I laughed out loud.

"Did he recognize you, Georgia?" I asked. "You probably see coyotes all the time out here. Have you chased him before?" I thought she probably had, by the way that gray skulker got himself out of there. Georgia felt bigger beneath me now, puffed up and proud of herself.

We turned the corner and rode toward the *Bosque,* which borders the western edge of Mimi's pasture. We crossed a stretch of tall, dun-colored grasses, heading toward the trees. They looked green-gold against the blue sky. The sun was low, and the trees cast long shadows into the pasture. I rode toward them. Even in late September, the afternoon was hot enough that shade seemed like a good idea.

Something moved in the grass a few hundred yards away. Georgia hesitated, pointing her ears at it. My fingers tightened around the saddle horn. *Another coyote,* I thought. But a small mule deer, the same color as the grasses, jumped up and bolted away from us. I felt Georgia swell up, like Picasso doing his parade gait. She took an eager step after the deer.

"No," I said, shortening the reins. "You're with me."

That had worked with the coyote, but not now. The deer soared over the far fence. Georgia snorted loudly, prancing and sidling. She even took a few cantering steps.

My heart raced as I tried to turn Georgia away from the deer. I made her do a figure eight, looping around first in one direction and then in the other. I gripped the reins and held my breath. *Please work, please work, please work,* I prayed.

By the second loop, Georgia's neck relaxed a bit. We did another loop. In the middle of it, Georgia heaved a huge sigh—and so did I.

"Good girl," I told her, letting my breath out in one big rush. "You're a good girl, Georgia."

When I looked up, I was relieved to see Luis jogging toward us on Picasso. I rode to meet him, still hearing my heart pounding in my ears.

"You handled that just right," he said. "You stayed in control and distracted her. I was hightailing over to the rescue, but that wasn't necessary."

I nodded and gave Luis a shaky smile. If he noticed how anxious I was, he didn't say. He turned Picasso in beside me, and we rode along the edge of the *Bosque,* gliding under golden cottonwoods and poplars.

When Luis stopped to straighten a post in the fence line, Georgia and I went on a few steps ahead. I couldn't stop thinking about the mule deer—how it had caught Georgia and me by surprise because of how it had blended in with the grass. As an artist, I'd always been drawn to bold colors. *But beige and brown are useful colors, too,* I thought, *if you don't want to be seen—or if you want to stand up suddenly and get someone's attention.*

I remembered the beige hallways at school, the ones we'd been trying to fill with colorful artwork, and suddenly I had an idea.

"That's it!" I said out loud.

Georgia's slender ears tilted back toward me.

"We'll dress in beige," I announced. "Get it, Georgia? A Day of Beige. We'll blend into the school walls and hold the most boring protest in the history of protests. We'll go invisible, like your deer! Then we'll stand up and show everyone how bland and boring life is for us without art. Get it?"

Georgia simply tossed her head.

Horses can be great friends, but sometimes you really need a human being. I couldn't wait to talk to Gabi and Tessa—even to Dylan, because going invisible was kind of like going on strike. She might even like this idea.

The next morning, Gabi and I met Tessa and Dylan at the classroom door. After coming up with my Day of Beige idea, I saw color popping out at me from every direction. Dylan wore an orange jersey. Tessa had on a blue-green shirt that looked great on her. I wore my red and black Navajo jacket, and Gabi wore a gauzy pink scarf. All the other kids wore bright colors, too. There was hardly any beige as far as the eye could see, except on the school walls and floor.

Good! If we pulled this off, it would be really noticeable.

As we hung up our jackets, I saw Dylan check out my outfit and raise her eyebrows a bit. I'd borrowed a tan T-shirt from Mom and tied a knot in the bottom so that it wouldn't be too big. I was hoping the boring shirt would help my friends understand my Day of Beige idea. So far, so good.

We huddled at our table. "Okay," I said. "Who had an idea?"

Gabi looked guilty. "I completely forgot," she admitted. Big surprise! All she had on her mind these days was dogs.

"I still think we should go on strike," Dylan said.

Tessa said, "I couldn't come up with anything. I didn't even have a dream last night."

"Well, how about this?" I said. *"Day of Beige!* It's kind of like a strike, Dylan—a color strike. We'll pick a day and get everybody who wants art in school to wear beige or tan—any color that blends in with the walls. It's like a statement. We'll remind teachers and the principal how not having art makes us feel—and how without art and color, we're kind of invisible."

"Will people notice?" Tessa asked thoughtfully.

"I would," I said.

"You're an artist!" Gabi said.

But Dylan's face lit up. "I know!" she said excitedly. "We'll get my mom to do a story on Day of Beige in the paper. We'll make sure people notice!"

"You want to do a story in the *newspaper?"* I asked, my stomach flip-flopping.

"How else are people going to find out about it?" Dylan asked. "If all we do is wear beige and show our teachers how not having art makes us feel, *nothing* will happen. We need to tell the rest of the city. That's what reporters do. Then maybe lots of people will read the story and want to help. Maybe we'll even find art teachers that way!"

The whole newspaper thing made my stomach

feel crawly. I looked around the table, hoping someone else felt nervous about it, too. But Tessa was nodding, and even Gabi seemed excited about a story in the paper. Before I could say anything else, Dylan had her phone out and was texting her mom.

"When should we do the Day of Beige?" I asked, trying to sound confident and take back control of the situation.

Dylan knew the answer to that, too. "The week before Balloon Fiesta starts," she announced.

"But that's next week!" I said. "That's too soon."

"Why?" Tessa asked. "It's not like a bake sale. All we have to do is put on different clothes—and tell everyone else to do the same thing."

I was suddenly annoyed with Tessa. Why did she have to keep taking Dylan's side? I looked to Gabi for support, but she just shrugged. The Dylan train had left the station, and there was no stopping it now.

Dylan opened her phone and pulled up a calendar. "Fiesta starts the first Saturday in October," she said. "That's the fifth this year—"

"So Monday, September 30th? Or Tuesday, October first?" Tessa asked.

"Tuesday," Dylan said. "Because we have to remind people. That would be a lot easier to do on

Monday than over the weekend. I'll tell my mom."
Dylan started texting again.

"But that's only"—I counted on my fingers—
"five days from now," I said. "There's no way!"

Gabi finally found her voice, too. "Maybe we
should slow down for a minute and make a solid
plan," she said.

Dylan glanced up from her phone. "What's
wrong with you guys?" she said. "You've both been
complaining for weeks that we don't have an after-
school art program yet. Here's our chance to do
something about it. What are you waiting for?"

I was speechless. I couldn't argue with Dylan's
point, much as I wanted to.

Just then Dylan got a text from her mother: *Day
of Beige on October 1. Luv it! I'll do the story.*

My stomach dropped.

Between classes, I did my part, telling other
students, "Wear beige next Tuesday to support after-
school art. Pass it on!" But secretly, I couldn't wait for
school to end so that I could talk to Mimi. If we were
making a mistake by rushing into this, Mimi would
tell me so, hopefully before it was too late.

That didn't happen. We were outdoors together, taking a short walk up and down the sidewalk in front of the rehab center. When she heard the words "Day of Beige," Mimi stopped walking and laughed out loud—a bigger and happier laugh than any I'd heard since her accident.

"That's *perfect!*" she said.

I was proud that Mimi liked my idea, but the newspaper thing was still making me nervous. "But do you think we need Dylan's mom to do a newspaper story?" I asked.

"Oh yes," Mimi said. "This is too good to keep to yourself. Besides, Saige, you do want to change things, don't you? That usually means going outside your comfort zone."

I looked at her, still pale from being indoors for weeks. A simple fall over a dog had taken Mimi way outside her comfort zone. Out of that, she'd learned a new drawing method and met a lot of new friends— yet she was still Mimi.

"Okay," I said. "Anyway, I think Dylan's the one who should be interviewed for the newspaper story. It's her mom who's the reporter."

Mimi raised her eyebrows. "I don't think so, Saige," she said gently. "You're the leader here. You came up with the idea, and you're probably the one who cares the most."

I stared back at Mimi. *True,* I thought. I did care the most. But . . . *man!* I guess I was stuck with this newspaper story thing—and it was all Dylan's fault!

Later, when I told Mom and Dad about Day of Beige, they loved the idea, too. "Sometimes you have to stand up for yourself," Dad said. "And what I like about this is, it's not a fight. It's a statement. It will make people laugh, and it will make them think. It doesn't get better than that."

Mom called Dylan's mom to learn more about the newspaper story. I listened to Mom's end of the conversation, which was mostly a lot of "mmm-hmms." It sounded as if Dylan's mom was just like Dylan. Mom couldn't get a word in edgewise.

After Mom finally hung up, she said that Dylan's mom was recommending a press conference. "Don't look so scared, Saige," she added reassuringly. "It's just a couple of local reporters asking a few questions, and luckily, you've planned this for a day when I have a light class schedule, so I'll be there to support you."

Mom explained how press conferences work. We needed to send an e-mail to all the local news organizations. That was called a press release, and Dylan's mother thought we should send it out first thing Tuesday morning, setting the press conference for noon at the school that day. I should prepare a statement to read and be ready to answer questions. That made my heart thunder. *What questions would the reporters ask? Would I know the answers? And what would the teachers at school say about all this? Would they get mad?*

"I'll review your statement if you want," Mom offered. "We could even do a mock press conference right here in the living room so that you can practice."

"Thanks, Mom," I said, but I was pretty sure I wouldn't want to practice. One press conference was going to be enough!

Worry gnawed at me all the next day, and I gnawed at my fingernails—but just a little, because of the looks I got at our table. Gabi looked worried for me, and Dylan said out loud just what she was thinking: "You're not freaking out, are you? Because this is not a big deal for you. Look at what you did with the Professor Picasso Show! You're a pro!"

"Not a big deal?" I practically squealed it, and I got a warning look from Mrs. Applegate. It was true that I'd done the Professor Picasso Show in front of a crowd of people, but I'd had Gabi and Picasso by my side. For some reason, this felt different—more scary and lonely, somehow. I thought about Mimi's words: *Change usually means going outside your comfort zone.* I was definitely stepping outside my comfort zone for the Day of Beige press conference, and right now all I wanted to do was jump back inside.

Saturday Gabi and I went to the neighborhood thrift shop to look for beige clothes. We scored big at the two-dollar rack, where Gabi found a shirt and I got a corduroy skirt. In the checkout line, I found a bandanna, too. You can find anything at that shop.

Afterward, Gabi, Luis, and I rode out into the *Bosque.* I knew I should stop worrying about the press conference, or Georgia would pick up on it. Horses can be very sensitive that way.

But Georgia pricked her ears at the trail ahead, less concerned about what was going on with me than with what was coming down the trail ahead. Someone was riding toward us on a bicycle. No big deal—except that Georgia had probably never seen a bicycle before. She'd gone rigid, and I was pretty sure she was holding her breath.

Here we go again, I thought, tensing my own body and flashing back to the mule deer incident.

But the biker—a woman in bright spandex and a helmet—seemed to understand what was going on. She turned around and biked a short distance in the other direction. The moment the bike was moving away from us, Georgia's body softened.

The woman veered off the path and parked her bike beneath a tree. Then she took a few steps toward the trail, as if waiting for us. "Hello," the woman called as we slowly approached. "Are these Mimi Copeland's Spanish Barbs?"

Luis groaned under his breath. "Oh boy!" he said to me, his voice low. "She found us. She called me last night, this lady—I don't know how she knew I'm a friend of Mimi's. She wants to buy one of the horses."

My heart sank like a stone thrown into the river. This woman wanted to buy Georgia—*my* Georgia.

I wanted to turn around and race back to Mimi's, but Georgia was fascinated by the bike. She took a deep breath and stepped toward it.

Picasso and Frida paid absolutely no attention to the bike. Picasso has been a parade horse and has seen hundreds of bikes. And Frida? An alien space-ship could land beside her, and she would just give it one of her sighs. But Georgia carried me helplessly up to the bicycle and the woman standing near it.

She was a tanned, middle-aged woman with short hair, and her eyes lit up as she looked at Georgia. "Beautiful!" she said, holding out the flat of her hand. Georgia sniffed it politely and then moved past it to look more closely at the bicycle.

The woman was excited, but she knew enough to use a soft voice. "This is my lucky day after all," she said to Luis. "I was so disappointed when I didn't find you out at the *ranchita*, but I remembered you saying you sometimes rode in the *Bosque,* and I thought it was worth a try. I finally have a place with enough land for horses, and I'm ready to buy my first Barb." Her eyes roamed over the three horses and settled on Georgia. "What a beautiful young mare! How old is she?"

I tried to remember. "Four, I think," I said in a near whisper.

"And steady enough to put a child on her?" the woman asked, looking impressed. My heart turned into a cold, sinking lump.

"Saige is an excellent rider," Luis said quietly. "And Georgia is becoming a fine riding horse."

"I can see that," the woman said. "Is she for sale?"

Gabi and I looked at each other in horror. It was supposed to be hard to sell horses these days! I'd been hoping it would take a long time for Mimi to find Georgia the perfect new owner—but this buyer had found us, right out here in the *Bosque.*

Luis answered the woman. He didn't exactly

say that Georgia was for sale, and he didn't exactly say that she wasn't. That didn't reassure me. I've seen Mimi horse-trading, and that's how it's done. You pretend you aren't really interested in selling. You're vague, but pleasant. You let the other person make the first move.

The woman asked for Mimi's phone number at the rehab facility. Luis said, "I'm sorry, but I don't feel comfortable giving you that."

"Then I'll give you my contact information," she said excitedly. "She can get in touch with me when she gets out."

Georgia ducked her head, asking for more rein, and started pawing the ground. I remembered Mimi saying, "Standing still is the hardest thing for a young horse to do." I should have made Georgia stop pawing, but I wasn't sure how. I glanced at the Bike Lady, wondering if she had noticed the pawing. *See?* I thought. *She's being bad. You don't want her.*

Luis noticed. "Why don't you girls ride on ahead?" he said. "I'll catch up with you in a minute." He turned politely back to the woman, who was hunting for a pen in her fanny pack.

I nudged Georgia with my heels. She broke into a canter. I wasn't sure I'd meant for her to do that, but

it felt great to get away from Bike Lady and all her
questions. Before we reached the bend in the trail,
I reined Georgia in, and Gabi came up beside me on
Picasso. We just looked at each other. Gabi's eyes were
wide and dark and worried.

I looked back up the trail. The lady was leaning
over, scribbling something on a tiny piece of paper.
"I wish we hadn't come riding today," I said.

"She would have found us at the *ranchita*, then,"
Gabi said. "She seems nice, doesn't she?" Gabi said
that like it was a bad thing, which it kind of was.
"I mean—she really understands horses. The way she
turned that bike around . . ."

I couldn't answer Gabi. If I said a word, I might
start crying.

We went on around the bend in the trail. After
a few minutes, Georgia paused and turned her head,
and Luis and Frida came into sight. We waited for
them.

Luis flashed me a sympathetic smile. "Don't
look so miserable, Saige," he said. "Mimi doesn't let
go of her horses easily, and never to anything less
than the perfect home. I'm not sure she's going to like
this lady. And even if she does, Mimi won't decide
anything until she's home and back on her feet."

Day of Beige

But Mimi was getting better every day.
I had never imagined I could possibly feel bad
about that.

Monday at school, Gabi, Tessa, Dylan, and
I had a scary job to do. Miss Fane was in on our
secret, and she thought we should tell the principal,
Mrs. Laird, about the press conference. "School rules,"
Miss Fane said. "If you don't tell the principal, the
press conference won't happen."

So Monday at lunchtime, the four of us walked
together in one brave line, taking up the whole hallway, to the principal's office. "We have something
important to tell Mrs. Laird," I told the secretary, and
a few minutes later we were in the inner office, and
Mrs. Laird was looking at us curiously.

I glanced at my friends, wondering what to say.
But they were all looking at me. "You're the leader,"
Mimi had said. I guess my friends felt the same way.
I took a deep breath.

"Tomorrow we're doing a . . . a protest," I said.
"A Day of Beige. We . . . we want to remind everyone
how boring life is without color and art, and how
much we really need our afternoon art class."

Mrs. Laird looked startled. "The after-school art program?" she said. "But I'm moving forward on that!"

"*When?*" Dylan burst out. "It's *October* already." She sounded angry, and I could tell she wanted to say more. Leaning forward in her chair, Dylan suddenly reminded me of Georgia that day in the pasture, tugging at the reins, eager to chase that mule deer.

Had Dylan said too much already? Mrs. Laird looked sharply at her and started to respond, but then pressed her lips together and said nothing.

I was getting scared. I shot a glance at Gabi. She'd been right. Being negative and making people feel bad didn't work.

Gabi cleared her throat. "The reporters will probably want to talk with you about the after-school class," she said calmly.

"Reporters?" Mrs. Laird asked sharply.

I gulped. "Tomorrow we'll all wear beige to school, and . . . at lunchtime, we're having a press conference. D-Dylan's mom is helping us."

Mrs. Laird frowned thoughtfully at Dylan, and then at the rest of us. She didn't say anything right away, and the silence made me squirm.

Then she nodded. "All right, girls," she said.

"I can see that you're serious about this, and I respect that. I'll let the administrators know, and we'll set up an area for the press conference and a process for registering reporters at the office. But will you allow me to say a few words tomorrow?"

How could we say no? I nodded, and Mrs. Laird stood up from behind her desk, her signal that we were dismissed.

"Thank you," Gabi said earnestly, and we echoed her. "Thanks." "Thank you."

"Whew!" I said, when we were a long way down the hall. "Gabi, you're not just a dog trainer. You're a lion tamer!"

"She was a little annoyed," Gabi agreed. "But at least she agreed to it."

"She was kind of cool about it, actually," said Tessa.

Only Dylan was silent. I wondered if she felt guilty about getting Mrs. Laird all riled up.

All afternoon we reminded everyone: Tuesday is Day of Beige. The kids we told, told other kids. The whole school was whispering, *"Beige." "Tomorrow." "Wear beige."*

I got ready for bed that night feeling sure
that I wouldn't be able to sleep. Other kids were just
making a wardrobe choice. I would have to talk to
reporters, and I didn't think my prepared statement
was all that brilliant. It didn't help that every time I
closed my eyes, I saw the face of that woman on the
bike, looking excitedly at my Georgia.

So I tried to keep my eyes open, and I was wide
awake when the phone rang. I was surprised when
Mom came to my door. "It's Tessa," she said. "It's very
late for a phone call, but just this once, it's okay." I sat
up in bed as she handed me the phone.

"Saige?" Tessa asked, sounding excited. I was
surprised by how good it felt to hear her voice on the
other end of the line.

"I found the perfect quote for you to read
tomorrow!" Tessa went on without waiting for me to
respond. "It was in one of my music books—I found
it by accident." I heard a page rustle, and then Tessa
read, "'Life without music can only be seen in black
and white. It takes music to add the color.' That's by
Artie Shaw."

"But we're not doing black and white," I said.
"We're doing beige."

"So change the quote," Tessa said. "Say 'art and

music.' Say 'beige.' Tell them that you've changed the quote."

"I could do that," I said slowly. "'Cause you're right—it's perfect, and it's what we really needed. Hey, thanks!"

"You're welcome," Tessa said. "I'll see you tomorrow."

As I set down the phone, I smiled to myself—in the dark, but not so alone anymore. *Tessa will be there with me tomorrow,* I reminded myself. And she had just made my prepared statement a whole lot better.

The next morning I met Gabi at our front door. She wore khaki pants, her "new" sand-colored shirt, and a huge grin. "Wow!" she said, checking out my outfit. "If you stand next to the school walls, nobody will even see you!"

She was right. I had on Mom's tan shirt and the beige corduroy skirt I'd found at the thrift shop. Even my shoes were tan. I'd braided my hair, wrapped it around my head, and covered it with my tan bandanna. My face would blend into the wall, too. I was pale with nervousness this morning. But seeing Gabi in "uniform," too, made me feel a little better.

We walked Sam and Rembrandt, as usual. But this morning, the dogs' black and white coats looked brilliant compared to us, and the sky above seemed especially blue. A gorgeous balloon drifted overhead, a yellow one with an orange *Zia* symbol—the sun symbol that's on the New Mexico flag. We noticed sunflowers, bright red tomatoes, and orange gourds in people's front gardens. The whole world was showing off this morning and helping us make our point.

Later, as we got to school, I saw the buses unloading a stream of kids in all shades of dullness—beige, tan, khaki, and desert camouflage. I felt a spike of excitement. Day of Beige was working! The first part, anyway. There was hardly anyone who hadn't gotten the message or who had forgotten. Just one or two bright shirts stood out in the flood of sandy-colored kids.

In the classroom, we all laughed at one another. Between the beige clothes and the bland walls, the room looked like a desert landscape.

Mrs. Applegate, working at her desk, looked up once and frowned, as if she was trying to figure something out. A few minutes later she looked up again and did a double take. "What's with the color scheme?" she asked Gabi, who sat nearest to her.

Gabi looked at me, startled. We hadn't figured out what to say if a teacher asked about our outfits. I answered for Gabi. "It's . . . a surprise!" I said. "Just wait—you'll see."

"A surprise? Hmm," said Mrs. Applegate, looking us over thoughtfully. "Teachers don't always like surprises."

My stomach flip-flopped. Clearly Mrs. Laird hadn't said anything yet to the teachers. Was Mrs. Applegate going to be mad at us?

I worried about that as the clock ticked overhead. Had the press release gone out this morning as planned? When would the reporters start gathering? The words kept repeating in my head: *Press conference. Press conference.* When the lunch bell finally rang, I jumped, like Georgia shying.

"You'll do fine," Tessa whispered. She, Gabi, and Dylan walked with me, all of us arm in arm, out into the sun. Several vans stood outside the school, with satellite dishes on top and the logos of TV and radio stations on the sides. A group of people, bristling with microphones, stood watching the school door.

I was relieved to see Dylan's mother in the group, and even more relieved when Mom's car pulled up. She was alone. Mimi was with another group of people, off to one side. No wheelchair anymore. She stood with her left hand resting lightly on her walker, looking around and enjoying the fresh air. When she spotted me, she waved and poked Celeste, from her oil painting group. I could lip-read what Mimi was saying: "There's Saige." She looked really proud.

Miss Fane was with them, too. She crossed the pavement and handed me a sheet of paper. "Some ammunition, if you need it," she said. "Good luck!" The paper was filled with facts on how art helps students. This would definitely come in handy! I gripped the paper tightly in my hands.

Now Dylan's mother came forward. She showed me where to stand and how to turn on my microphone. Then she gave me an encouraging smile and stepped back. I pulled my prepared statement out of the pocket of my skirt and unfolded it carefully.

"Than—" I cleared my throat. "Thank you for coming. My name is Saige Copeland, and I'm in fourth grade. I have something to read, and then I'll take some questions." I cleared my throat again. "Okay."

I started reading. I was so glad for Tessa's

quote. It was an important person saying the same thing we were trying to say today.

"'Life without art or music is beige,'" I read. "'It takes art, and music, to add the color.' That's a quote from the musician Artie Shaw. I changed it a little, but it really says what we're trying to say here."

I looked up at the microphone booms and the reporters scribbling in their notebooks. "This protest is called Day of Beige," I went on. Everybody laughed, which was encouraging. "We all wore beige today to show what school is like for us when we don't have art class. We know it's hard to get a program like this started, but it's important."

I looked down at my paper and took a deep breath. This was the hardest part. "A few weeks ago we raised a lot of money for an after-school art class, but it's taking a lot of time to organize," I said. "We're just saying please, please, hurry."

That was my whole statement. I looked out at the reporters. They raised their hands, as if I were a teacher and they were the students, and shouted out my name. I called on Dylan's mom first.

She smiled encouragingly. "Day of Beige is such a great name for an arts protest," she said. "Where did you get the idea?"

"Out riding, actually," I answered. "My horse and I were surprised by a mule deer that blended in with the brown grass, and Day of Beige just popped into my head." That got a laugh, and all the reporters scribbled in their notebooks.

"Why is it so important to you to have art classes at school?" a reporter asked.

I looked down at the paper in my hands. "Ammunition," Miss Fane had called it. I read, "Kids who have art do better in academic subjects and score higher on tests. We don't drop out of school as much. We concentrate better, so we do better in *all* of our classes."

"Can you tell us more about the after-school art class?" another reporter asked.

"Well, we haven't had it yet," I said, "so I don't know . . ."

"Maybe I can answer that," Mrs. Laird said. She came to the microphone and talked about how an after-school class could be structured, with a professional art teacher or two, volunteer helpers, and a regular teacher to stay after school to help supervise.

Then Mrs. Laird was asked about her response to the demonstration. She answered carefully. "The kids were very respectful, I have to say that," she said.

"And I agree with Saige about time. It's taken longer than I had hoped to pull this program together. But we've all heard what the kids are saying, and I hope to get this program off the ground by November at the latest."

A TV camera swiveled toward me as she said "November." I'm sure it caught a very disappointed expression. But right away, the reporters had more questions for me.

Why did I like art? one reporter asked.

Why did I like art? I didn't even know where to begin. I thought of Mimi's studio, my favorite place in the whole world, and of how it felt to sit beside her, bringing something from my imagination to life on canvas. I thought of the paintings Mimi and I had created there, and of the horses we'd watched through the window—wise Picasso and beautiful young Georgia. At the thought of her, I felt my chest swell. I couldn't speak.

Luckily, someone else could. "Art is like music," I heard someone say, and I glanced over to see Dylan, bold Dylan, stepping up to the microphone to help me out. "It helps us express what we feel inside."

Gabi was there, too, and Tessa, and when I glanced over my shoulder, I saw a solid beige wall of classmates standing behind me. There were so many of them, way more than I'd ever expected. They all thought art was worth fighting for, just as I did. I couldn't believe what we had done—together.

"Art brings us together," I said, finding my voice. "When I create art, especially with my friends, I feel like . . . anything is possible."

There was a moment of silence. Then someone started clapping, which led to more applause, so I said, "Thank you. Thank you for coming!" I stepped back from the microphone, and that ended the Day of Beige press conference.

It was strange seeing myself on TV. I looked young and small in front of the microphone, and my voice was shaky sometimes. But we had gotten on TV! The news anchors loved saying "Day of Beige," and they mentioned all the stuff I'd said about how art helps kids. And the next morning we were in the newspaper, with "Day of Beige" as the headline.

We didn't plan it, but that day everyone wore something bright to school. Our classroom looked like a Mass Ascension at Balloon Fiesta.

"Look at Mrs. Applegate," Gabi whispered.

She was colorful, too, today in a green short-sleeved sweater that glittered when she moved.

"*All* the teachers are wearing something sparkly," Gabi said. "Come on, let's get a drink of water before the bell rings. I'll show you."

Tessa and Dylan came, too. Something felt different among us today, as if the four of us were a true team. As annoyed as I'd been with Dylan last week, I had to admit that her bold ideas had made the protest a lot more powerful.

We hurried down the hall, peeking into each classroom we passed. Every teacher was wearing something sparkly, even the men. Mr. Jimenez had on a broad silver and turquoise belt buckle. Mr. Alvarez wore his Christmas tie with flashing LED lights.

When the bell rang, we rushed back to class—past Mrs. Laird, standing outside her office. She sparkled, too, in a green silky scarf that gleamed with silver threads, and I'm pretty sure she smiled at me.

After calling the class to attention, Mrs. Applegate made a little speech. "You may have noticed something about the teachers this morning," she said. "The sparkly clothes we're wearing are our sign to you. We heard you yesterday. You've re-ignited a spark in us, our own passion for the arts, and we're going to do something about it."

"Yay!" I whispered, clapping my hands once before I could stop myself. Mrs. Applegate smiled.

"We're meeting with Mrs. Laird and the district administration this afternoon about the after-school art program," she continued. "I have heard that after yesterday's protest, several people came forward to volunteer to teach and help out with the program. But it may still take time to create, and not every student will be able to stay after school to take part. So we'll also try to bring more art into our regular classes. In math, for instance, we'll explore geometric shapes through quilt design."

"*Yes!*" somebody said across the room.

"In history," Mrs. Applegate said, "I'm assigning you each a research project. You'll choose some aspect of New Mexico history and do an illustrated report, or—yes, Saige—an art project, or—yes, Tessa!—a music project." Sometimes it's scary how well Mrs. Applegate knows us.

Mrs. Applegate had us write lists of everything we'd learned about the history of New Mexico so that we could pick a topic. She walked around the room, making suggestions. "Interesting," she said when we were done. "Given the chance to do a fun project, you remember more about New Mexico's history than your quiz results suggest. I can't wait to see what you all do!"

Me neither. I looked around the room and thought, *I like school!* That's not how I'd felt back in August, but school was different now. *We* were different. We'd done something big, all of us together. And I was the one who'd gotten the ball rolling, with an idea that had come to me while out riding Georgia.

Then it hit me—the best idea ever for a history-art project, and it was all about Georgia.

I couldn't wait to tell Mimi, but when we got to the rehab center that afternoon, she had news of her own. She held up a bare, white, skinny arm. "Look!

95

No cast!" she exclaimed, flashing her brilliant Mimi smile. "They tell me I can go home Friday."

"Friday?" I almost shrieked. Just in time for the Balloon Fiesta!

Mom smiled. Mimi must have given her a heads-up about this.

"I'm so looking forward to being in my own home and my own bed," Mimi said. She glanced out at the busy hallway, full of people who were all so familiar by now. "I wonder if I'll feel lonely at first."

"What about Rembrandt?" I asked.

Mimi sighed. "Could he stay with you for the first week or two?" she asked Mom.

"Good idea," Mom said firmly. "The last thing you need is to trip over him again!"

Mimi had everything else under control. A cousin of Carmen's who did home-health work would look in on her once a day for the first week or two. A physical therapist would come to the *ranchita* three times a week. Luis would visit Mimi first thing every morning, and we would look in on her in the evenings.

So this was one of the last afternoons I'd spend at the rehab center. I felt a tiny bit sad as I collected our paintings and smocks from the art room and carried a few of Mimi's personal things out of her room. I was getting Mimi back, but I was losing something, too—doing art with this group and seeing Miss Fane. I hoped the rehab center would figure out how to keep its art program going. But they would have to work on that themselves. I had an after-school art program to keep moving in the right direction.

What would it be like, having Mimi back at the *ranchita*? And with Mimi getting on with her regular life, would I lose Georgia soon? I couldn't think about that right now. Mimi was coming home. Mimi was coming *home. Finally!*

On Friday, I rode the bus to the *ranchita,* just like in the old days. Mimi didn't come to the door, but I heard her voice when I pushed open the latch. "Good!"

A huge lump rose in my throat. I'd waited so long for this—Mimi home again. Life getting back to normal.

Mimi sat on the couch in the studio. She had the kitten in her lap. I could hear the purring all the way across the room.

"I've decided to name her Stella," Mimi told

me. "After Frank Stella, the abstract artist."

"But he's a man!" I protested.

"Stella's a nice name," Mimi said. "And she's a nice little cat. We've enjoyed spending some time together today. Luis and Carmen were here earlier, but I sent them home."

Mimi pushed the kitten gently off her lap and stood up, pretty slowly and with support from the arm of the couch. She reached for her cane and walked stiffly to the easels, where my purple impasto painting and her pink horses still waited.

"We've both been through quite a bit since we last worked on these," Mimi said. "I've been looking and thinking, do I still want to do this picture?"

I felt uneasy. Mimi was back, but things weren't the same. She hadn't just come in from working a horse, for one thing. Looking at her walk, I wasn't sure when that would happen. And Mimi hardly ever second-guesses a painting. She believes that artists finish things.

Still, I knew what she meant. These pictures felt like a long time ago.

"I still want you to finish yours," I said.

"And I want you to finish yours," Mimi said. "I don't know why you thought you were in a rut,

Saige. That looks unlike anything I've ever seen you paint before."

I flushed a little and looked at the painting again. Yes, I could feel it calling to me, telling me what to do next.

But I had something else in mind: my history project for Mrs. Applegate. I had decided to paint Georgia posed against a New Mexico sky, carrying a *conquistador*.

I dug out a fresh canvas and started sketching it all out. The Georgia part was easy. I had been looking at her, grooming her, riding her, and thinking about her for weeks now. The rider was harder. I kept making him too small—my size. And I didn't know enough about the armor that *conquistadores* wore.

Mimi pointed me toward some of her big art books. I dragged them out and we huddled over them, sketching and scribbling notes. I was way into my project, but every once in a while, I'd hear a chicken outside or one of the horses moving, and I'd realize—*Mimi's here! We're here together!*

Mom and Dad both came to Mimi's that afternoon. They brought groceries and cooked supper, and we celebrated. It seemed perfectly normal, except when Mimi got up to do something simple like use the bathroom. She was so slow, so careful, and her cane tapped along the floor, a completely new sound in the house. Were we really going to leave her all by herself?

"Do you want me to stay overnight?" I asked Mimi while we were eating dessert.

"No," she said quickly. "You'll want to get to the Balloon Fiesta first thing in the morning."

Mimi was right. But I knew I wouldn't be able to enjoy the fiesta, not if I was worrying that Mimi had fallen again. "We can watch the Mass Ascension from here in the morning," I said. "And I can go over to the park later."

Mimi looked hard at me. Then she looked across the table at Mom and Dad, who nodded their approval. "All right," she said abruptly. "I'll admit, I was just a little nervous at the idea of being alone tonight. Yes, please do stay, Saige!"

After supper, Dad and Mimi washed dishes. Mom and I put fresh sheets on Mimi's bed and made up the guest room bed for me. It was nice to be with Mom, making a bed. It made me feel grown up.

"So what about your birthday?" Mom asked out of the blue. "Are you and Tessa going to do your usual balloon flight?"

I started to say yes, but the image of our class-room table popped into my mind: Tessa, Gabi, and Dylan. *All* my friends were at that table—except Mimi, my best friend of all. Then the ideal birthday celebration popped into my head, just as Day of Beige had.

"I want to do something different this year," I said. "Could I have a party? A real party, with more than one friend, at Fiesta? There's plenty of space to set up tables there. And there are already balloons— we won't need party balloons! Just a cake, maybe."

"I think we could manage that," Mom said with a smile. "What about your balloon ride?"

That was the big one. "Do you think Mimi could come up with me?" I asked. "Because she's the one I'd really like to have."

Mom looked thoughtful. "That's a wonderful idea," she said. "Why don't you ask Mimi herself? She'll probably want to check with her doctor, but I think her leg has healed very well, and she couldn't have a better pilot!"

"No, Dad's the best," I agreed.

Mom kissed the top of my head. "I'm glad you're staying here tonight. As you know"—she sighed—"your dad and I will be up *very* early and out at the park for Mass Ascension. Call me on my cell when you both get up."

After Mom and Dad left, Mimi turned to me. "Ready for bed?" she asked. "I'm exhausted." But her eyes sparkled when she added, "I'm setting the alarm for five o'clock. We'll get up and watch the Dawn Patrol!"

Dawn Patrol is much earlier than the Mass Ascension. Mom would say it was crazy to get up for it, and not just because *she* hates early mornings. Mom would think that Mimi should be resting and healing instead. But I thought it was a great idea!

I wasn't quite as thrilled when the alarm clock rang the next morning. But I'm a balloonist's daughter. I put my clothes on over my pajamas and threw on my jacket. It really helps to be warm if you're up early.

Then I helped Mimi find warm things to wear. It took some digging. Back in August, when she fell, we were all wearing warm-weather clothes. But I found her a sweater and made cups of tea. We went out onto the shadowy porch, settled into our chairs, and looked out across the dark horse pasture. The sky was a deep, brilliant blue, a magical color. I checked the time on my cell phone. No point calling Mom and Dad yet. It was 5:35. They'd be very busy.

We waited, sipping our tea. Picasso, pearl-white in the dawn light just like in my painting, came to the water tub for a drink, followed by the rest of the herd.

"Hello, horses," Mimi said quietly.

Picasso lifted his head sharply and looked toward the porch. Then he nickered. Behind him, Frida nickered, too. "Now that's a surprise!" Mimi said. "Frida, I didn't know you cared."

Georgia was hard to see in the half-darkness— just a shadowy shape, as if she was already a memory. I felt panic rising in my chest, but then I remembered my painting of her in Mimi's studio. If I could finish that painting before Mimi sold Georgia, I would *never* forget my beautiful horse. I'd have to hurry.

"Look!" said Mimi, interrupting my thoughts. To the east, a glowing orange teardrop rose above the horizon. Another followed, a red and black checker-board. Then came a third, and that was Dad. I could see the spiral swirl of colors that Mimi had designed for his balloon.

"*Beautiful!*" Mimi breathed.

We sat right there on the porch through Dawn Patrol, and then the Mass Ascension. We watched balloon after balloon come up, as if a giant beyond the horizon were blowing soap bubbles. After a few minutes, Mimi reached over and took my left hand in her right. Her grip was weaker than it used to be, from being in the cast, but it was strong enough. Plenty strong enough.

It was the beginning of a perfect Balloon
Fiesta—or Saige Fiesta, as we like to call it—and a
perfect birthday week. Mimi loved the idea of going
up in the balloon with me. "I've been cooped up for
so long," she said. "Getting up into the sky is exactly
what I need! I'll just have to clear it with my doctor."

And I'll have to clear it with Tessa, I thought.

Monday morning before school started, I asked
my three friends to my party. Dylan looked surprised
and pleased, Gabi just looked pleased, and Tessa
looked as if she had a question she wanted to ask me.
I knew what it was, and I answered it, trying to be as
bold as Georgia and Dylan. "I'm asking Mimi to go
on my balloon ride this year," I announced.

Now *Tessa* looked pleased. "Awesome!" she
said. "I wondered what you were going to do." I saw
her glance awkwardly at Gabi, and I knew what she
was thinking. She was probably disappointed about
not going up in the balloon, but relieved that I hadn't
asked Gabi instead of her. A lot had changed between
Tessa and me lately, but our friendship was still strong.
I smiled our special cat smile at her, and she smiled
back.

All week long I went back and forth between the *ranchita* and Balloon Fiesta Park, getting huge doses of balloon color and festivity, and huge doses of Mimi.

And painting. Mimi couldn't sit long at her easel—it made her bones ache. But she'd get up, roam, rub her wrist, and come back to the Sandia horses while I worked on my painting of Georgia.

"You've really gotten to know her," Mimi said one afternoon, looking over my shoulder. "You've caught that bold, independent spirit of hers—just like Georgia O'Keeffe's. And like yours, Saige. You have a bold spirit, too."

Do I? I wondered. I'd never thought of myself as bold—bold like Georgia, or like Dylan.

Mimi caught my hesitation. "Think of all you've accomplished in the last couple of months, Saige," she said.

I thought of the arts fund-raiser—leading the parade on Picasso and doing the Professor Picasso act with Gabi. I thought of organizing Day of Beige and of speaking at the press conference. And I thought of Mrs. Laird's announcement just this morning that the after-school arts program would start in only two weeks. *Two weeks!*

Maybe I *was* bold. Maybe Georgia had rubbed off on me. Maybe while I was training her, she had trained me a little bit, too.

If I was so bold, then I should ask Mimi the question that had lurked beneath everything this past week, the question I'd hardly dared think about. "That lady who wanted to buy a Spanish Barb," I finally blurted. I'd never mentioned her to Mimi, but I was sure Luis had. "Did you ever get in touch with her?" I asked, holding my breath.

Mimi shook her head. "I need time to settle in and get my feet back under me before I think about that," she said.

So there was still time. I exhaled, and put a few finishing touches on Georgia's ears. The painting really did capture her spirit—and somehow, despite armor and a beard, the *conquistador* still looked a little like me. Georgia might never be mine, but at least in this painting, we'd always be together.

We held my birthday party at the Night Magic Glow, on the last weekend of Fiesta. As dusk settled in, Dad and a couple of hundred other balloonists inflated their envelopes and burned their jets. The balloons inflated against the deep-blue sky, the color of jewels—or the color jewels *should* be. I find gemstones kind of disappointing compared to a balloon Glow.

Mom set up lawn chairs and card tables in front of Dad's balloon. We gathered there with Mimi, Gabi, Tessa, Dylan, and even Luis and Carmen, who'd closed their booth an hour early to join my party.

I got a big notepad and a pen. "I'm ready to take your dinner orders," I announced with a grin. Balloon Fiesta is famous for its food booths, and there were a lot of them nearby.

We took everyone's orders and fanned out to the booths. Then we gathered again with pizza, green chile cheeseburgers, and so much more. Tessa and I have always loved turkey crepes, but I'd never tried *spanakopita*, a pastry filled with spinach and cheese. That was Gabi's favorite, and it was amazing. After one bite, I said, "Oh, Gabi, I'm so glad we're friends!"

Dylan's favorite was chocolate-dipped bacon. I didn't like that at first bite. I took a second nibble just to make sure. Hmm . . . and a third bite. "Wait, I *do* like it!" I said, surprised.

Dylan smiled across the card table at me, and I smiled back at her. We didn't need to say it out loud.

I hadn't liked Dylan at first, either, but now we were friends, too.

Then it was time for presents. Gabi gave me a clicker that I could wear on my wrist—it hung on a curly plastic bracelet. "For when you're riding," she said. "You can use it to train Georgia."

The birthday feeling sank for a moment, like the balloon when Dad turns the jets down. *I* wouldn't be training Georgia. That bike woman probably would. But I thanked Gabi all the same. Maybe I could use the clicker to help her train her new dog one day soon.

Dylan gave me a pair of earrings, my favorite shade of blue. How did she know? "Thank you!" I said with a smile.

I reached for Tessa's present next. It was small, too—definitely another piece of jewelry. I tore off the paper and opened the box.

"Oh, Tessa!" I exclaimed. It was the turquoise spoon ring that she'd made in class with Luis.

"It's to keep you safe out riding," Tessa said.

Another riding present led to another moment of sadness, but I swallowed it down. There were too many things to be thankful for today to waste any time feeling blue. "Thank you, Tessa," I said, giving her our special cat smile. I tucked the ring carefully back into the box.

Mimi said, "You're going to have to wait for my present."

That made sense. She hadn't been out shopping yet. "Having you *home* is my present," I told her.

Mimi flashed me a smile. "Oh, no, it's not!" she said. "I have something a lot better than that in store for you." She looked so pleased with herself that I got that birthday morning feeling all over again. What could Mimi's gift be? When would I get it? Tomorrow, maybe, before we went up in the balloon? Mimi's doctor had given her the clear for that. I couldn't wait!

But now it was time for cake. Mom had baked a sheet cake, and Carmen had decorated it with frosting hot-air balloons. I blew out my candles—all ten of them—in one fast puff, and then cut slices of cake for my friends. We sat there eating and looking out at the huge glowing balloons around us, tethered to the earth but still reaching toward the sky.

At eight o'clock the Glow ended. While Dad and the other balloonists were deflating and packing up their envelopes, the rest of us watched the fireworks. "Who else gets fireworks on their birthday?" Tessa said. "Happy birthday, Saige!"

The next day, Mom, Dad, Mimi, and I were back at Fiesta Park at the crack of dawn—*before* dawn, even. Dad was going up for the last Dawn Patrol, and Mimi and I would go with him.

Mom and I helped Dad prep and inflate the balloon while Mimi watched. She wore a leather jacket, cowboy chaps, and her heavy leather gauntlets that come halfway up to her elbows. "They'll keep the chill out," she said, "and if we have a little bump, they'll hold me together."

Mimi held a rectangular package under her arm, wrapped in the Sunday comics, Mimi's favorite gift wrap. She couldn't have gone shopping between last night and this morning. So what could the gift be? I'd find out soon enough.

We got into the basket, and Mimi settled herself in the one small chair. We watched as other balloons rose into the sky. Five minutes later, when Dad received his cue to launch, he tweaked the burners expertly and Mom untethered us.

We gently lifted off. First came the little tug as the envelope took the full weight of the basket and us. Then came the lightness, the rush as we rose,

swiftly and smoothly, into the dark-blue sky. There were more balloons around us. As we rose, Dad and the other pilots phoned back to the ground, reporting that there were no dangerous crosswinds—just a perfect Albuquerque Box. The lower-level winds were blowing north, and the ones higher up were blowing south, which meant the pilots could easily control where they went.

Soon we were high above the trees, above the radio towers. Dad completed his last transmission as we began to drift north and a little west—and then a little more west.

"At this rate we'll be over your house soon, Ma," said Dad.

I looked down. On the road below, I thought I saw our pickup truck. Mom was following us, probably rubbing sleep from her eyes. Up ahead the roofs looked familiar. There was Luis and Carmen's little house, and then Mimi's house and barn, and the giant cottonwoods, and the horse pasture.

The horses were out grazing. They looked up at us and then went back to eating, all except Georgia. She tossed her head playfully and galloped after the balloon's dark shadow, striking at it with her front feet. Brave Georgia. Beautiful Georgia.

My heart swelled, looking at her.

Mimi said, "There couldn't be a better time than this, Saige." She handed me my present. I could feel a frame beneath the wrapping, so it must be a picture. The Sandia horses had still been on Mimi's easel yesterday, and the paint hadn't had time to dry, so it wasn't that.

I started to tear the paper, still watching Georgia. She was showing off, circling the pasture with her black tail high, streaming out behind her. If that bike lady could only see her now . . .

I pushed that thought away, crumpled the paper into a ball, and stuffed it into my backpack, safely away from the jets. I was looking at the back side of one of Luis's beautiful tinwork frames. That was a present in itself.

I turned it over, and it wasn't a picture at all. It was an official-looking document with a gold seal. Georgia's name was on it, and the words *Spanish Barb Register*. Why was Mimi giving me this?

"This is the line you want to look at," Mimi said, pointing.

I read, *Owner: Saige Copeland.*

"But you're selling her!" My voice squeaked. "You said you were selling her!"

Mimi smiled. "No, I said she needed a new owner," she corrected me. "An owner who could give her the attention she deserves. Now she's got one!"

"But . . ." I said. *"Shouldn't* you sell her? I mean, to spread the word about Spanish Barbs?"

"You'll do that," Mimi said. "Take her out in the world. Show her off. Don't hesitate to mention who bred her—I still have other horses for sale! And someday you can breed her, maybe, and raise her foals."

I stared at Mimi, and then back at Georgia, already tiny in the distance. Georgia was *mine*?

Yes. It said so on this framed certificate with the gold seal.

"Wow," I said. "I mean—*thank* you! I mean—"

"I know exactly what you mean," Mimi said, smiling. Our eyes met, and I knew. She always did know what I meant, and she always would.

"Go back, Dad!" I said. "Can you go back? I need to look at my horse!"

Dad pulled the cord to release some hot air from the balloon. We slowly descended to catch the north wind—and fly back to Georgia.

Letter from American Girl

Dear Readers,

Saige and her friends discover that when they combine their creative talents, they can truly make a difference at school and in their community.

Here are the stories of four real girls who used their talents for painting and jewelry making to make a difference in their communities. Read their stories, and then learn how YOU can tap into your creativity to help others, too.

Your friends at American Girl

Helper of Birds

Olivia B. cried when she heard about an oil spill in the Gulf of Mexico and how it hurt birds such as terns and brown pelicans. "To me, birds are like angels," she says. "I couldn't let this happen, so I took action."

The New York 11-year-old wrote a letter to a national bird conservation group. She offered to draw portraits of birds that could be sold to raise money for bird rescue and rebuilding wetlands. The organization liked her idea, and over the next three months, Olivia created 500 original bird drawings. Her efforts raised more than $180,000, which was used for coastal cleanup and bird-habitat restoration.

"This is our planet," says Olivia. "We have to make it work for ourselves and for the animals. We can't move to Mars—and they can't, either."

She likes frogs, too!

Some of Olivia's artwork

← Little
Airplane
charm

Furry
Friends
charm →

Charms for Charity

Kyra H. knows a lot about helping others— even how to help by shopping! "In the grocery store, my mom showed me how buying cookies made by a particular company helps people because the company donates money to charity," the California girl says.

So Kyra, age 10, decided to raise money that way, too. She sculpted five different charms out of clay, each one to benefit a specific charity. The designs were made into silver charms for necklaces. Selling them through her mom's jewelry store, she raised almost $3,000.

Kyra donated money from her paw-shaped Furry Friends charm to an animal shelter. Her Little Airplane charm raised money to fly doctors to a health clinic in Mexico. "My parents taught me that even if you're young, helping others is a good thing to do," Kyra says.

119

Cute Crafts

When Rachel E. and Naomi G. first started making tiny cupcake earrings, the cute jewelry was a big hit. "A lot of girls at school liked our earrings," says Naomi, age 11. "So we decided to have a craft sale."

The girls sculpted, baked, and painted tons of tiny charms—cute cupcakes, itty-bitty bananas, even adorable little asparagus spears. They used the charms to make earrings, bracelets, and necklaces. "Making doughnut charms and painting on frosting and sprinkles is my favorite," says Rachel, also 11.

Along with their jewelry for sale, the Massachusetts friends displayed four large coffee cans for donations. "Each can was labeled for a specific organization. That way, customers could choose where their money went," explains Rachel. "We kept our prices really low so that everyone could afford them, and lots of people donated extra."

The girls raised more than $1,000 and donated it to four different charities. They also held a sale to benefit earthquake survivors in Haiti. "Sometimes people need help," says Naomi. "I'm glad I get to do craft sales and help others with Rachel. She's a great friend."

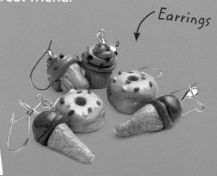

Earrings

Tokens of Thanks

When Haley K. heard the news about victims in Japan who had lost family members and homes during a devastating tsunami, she knew that she wanted to help. "I had gotten into making jewelry," Haley explains. "So I decided to make bracelets as a token of thanks for people who donated money."

Haley, her parents, her brother, and her friends made more than 500 colorful beaded bracelets. Each one had a red bead in the center to symbolize Japan's flag and hope for the victims. Haley got donations from neighbors, school friends,

dancers at her studio, and many others. The bracelets helped Haley raise more than $4,000 for tsunami victims.

"Before this experience, I didn't know how to help out in a crisis," says the Massachusetts nine-year-old, who gave all the money to a tsunami relief group that helped victims with medical care and other needs. "The best part was hearing how the money was used to help victims in Japan," Haley says. "I loved helping to make a difference."

Haley selling her bracelets

Hold Your Own Craft Sale

A craft sale is a great way to get creative with friends and raise money for a good cause.* Follow these tips to help make your sale a success!

Choose a cause. Brainstorm ideas with friends. Then ask a parent to help you choose a charity that supports that cause. Consider these:
• Feeding the hungry
• Caring for homeless animals
• Helping victims of a natural disaster
• Protecting endangered species

Pick your craft. Consider making or decorating . . .
• greeting cards.
• friendship bracelets.
• hair accessories.
• picture frames.
• holiday decorations.

Pick your place.
• Ask a parent if you can hold the sale in your garage or outside.
• Ask your principal if your school can host a craft fair.
• Find out whether a local church or community center is holding a craft show or holiday bazaar.

Set your price. Charge at least twice as much as you spent on supplies for each craft. If you spent twenty dollars on supplies for ten bracelets, each cost two dollars to make. A fair price per bracelet is four dollars.

* Some states may require you to register certain fund-raising activities. Please ask a parent to help you research the rules for your state.

Make a date. If you're holding your own sale, schedule it for a weekend, when you'll have more customers. Make signs advertising the sale and the charity you're supporting.

Be safe. Ask an adult to help out on the day of your sale. Keep your cash out of sight, in a safe place, and as soon as your sale is done, donate the profits to your advertised charity.

For more craft sale tips, look for the book *Express Yourself* by Emma MacLaren Henke.

craft Sale

Jessie Haas grew up loving horses, drawing horses, riding horses, and reading every horse book she could find—so it's no wonder that when she began writing, most of her 36 books turned out to be about horses. She's written picture books, easy readers, historical novels, poetry, and nonfiction.

Jessie has always trained her own horses, a job made easier and more fun when she discovered clicker training. She also loves to ride, knit, cook, write stories, and read.

Jessie lives in a solar-powered cabin next door to the Vermont farm she grew up on. She shares her home with her husband, Michael J. Daley (also a children's book author), two cats, a dog, and an adventurous hen. Her brave and opinionated Morgan horse, Robin, lives on the family farm, along with a small herd of Irish Dexters, a rare breed of cattle.

Learn more about Jessie at www.jessiehaas.com.